HURRICANE SISTERS

HURRICANE SISTERS

TALES OF LOW COUNTRY LADIES

J. C. FEWELL

iUniverse, Inc.
Bloomington

Hurricane Sisters
Tales of Low Country Ladies

iUniverse books may be ordered through booksellers or by contacting:

iUniverse
1663 Liberty Drive
Bloomington, IN 47403
www.iuniverse.com
1-800-Authors (1-800-288-4677)

ISBN: 978-1-4759-5296-4 (sc)
ISBN: 978-1-4759-5298-8 (hc)
ISBN: 978-1-4759-5297-1 (e)

Library of Congress Control Number: 2012918894

Printed in the United States of America

iUniverse rev. date: 10/09/2012

In memory of the original Hurricane Sisters: Marge, Mimi, and Yvonne.

Special thanks to my hurricane sister, Denise, and her mamma, Ida.

Since the 1980s, volunteers from Help Mobil Meals have fanned out over Beaufort, SC, delivering hot meals to the elderly, shut-ins, and patients recently discharged from Beaufort Memorial Hospital. The story "The Possum Laughed" was inspired by their service and the dedication of the coordinator, Beth Moon. Thanks to them for their service.

Also, a million thanks are due to my copyeditor, proofreader, and husband, Howard. Stephanie Austin Edwards and members of my writing group are full of patience and prudence, all fine Low Country Ladies.

CONTENTS

Note xi

Sissy's Storm 1

The Eye of the Storm. 7

Haint Blue 19

Boy in a Storm 21

Mare's Tales and Mackerel Skies 37

Shrimp and Pan-Fried Grits. 54

The Possum Laughed. 57

Mozelle's Market 74

Kate's Progress. 77

Hurricane Season 87

The Marine Corps Birthday Storm 89

Background. 101

NOTE

A great debate has taken place in my writing group about the way Gullah and Low Country speech should be written. The risk is to sound patronizing or disrespectful. It must be left to the reader's imagination then to hear the sweet, gentle Gullah pronunciation and the white folks' drawl, with three exceptions: *you all* is spelled *y'all*, the *g* is dropped from *ing* endings, and the verb *be* is used with joy and abandon.

Now, someone explain how Massachusetts folks mismanage those *r's* ....

The *Come-Heres* (it sounds more like *come yeres* or *come yahs*) are folks who were not born in the Low Country. It doesn't matter how long you have lived in Beaufort County, whether you came down in 1863 or 1963, *ya ain't born yere, ya ain't been yere, ya ain't from yere*. And don't you forget it.

For more information about Gullah voices, please visit Penn Center on St. Helena Island, South Carolina. As Mr. Leroy says, "It's not the end of the earth; it's the center."

Photo by Howard R Harris

SISSY'S STORM

AUGUST 21, 2017

Sissy Forester Merrill finally came home. She had ignored the tropical storm stirring the warm waters near Santo Domingo. Her mother, Kate, had always said it was during the years ending in a nine that you needed to watch the winds sweeping over the Sahara and off Cape Verde. That was when the great rain engine took a bead on the Atlantic Coast. The curse of the nines, she called it.

Besides, it was a La Niña year. Atlantic hurricanes were supposed to be absent in those conditions. Sissy was confident her mother's unrented house was safe. In fact, the little town of Elijah's Landing smugly sat in the little bite of coastline between Savannah and Charleston, safe haven since 1959.

The neighborhood in Elijah's Landing, ten years after World War II, was inhabited by navy chiefs, sergeant majors, and warrant officers plus the civilian firemen. As the locals on the Little Dog Key say, "Some folk *been here;* some folk *come here.*" The military families all *come here.* Or come back here.

The military wives held things together. Her dad always said, "They also serve who stand and wait." That tradition made them sisters, though not blood. The military traditions, the storms, and well, Charlie Hall, the weatherman forecasting out of Charleston sealed the stormy bonds of sisterhood.

1

The wives had spent all their married lives packing and moving to some forsaken port or post. Now each had a house that could be called home—a place to put down roots. Kate Forester wanted to put a sign out front that read, "Done Moving." But Sissy's dad still starched and at attention, wouldn't let her.

Ted Forester bought their first television and got on the roof to aim the antenna at Charleston so he could get the weather forecast and Walter Cronkite. Walter and Charlie, they were friends of the family. They stopped by each evening at six o'clock.

Well, all that was gone. Sissy needed to get her bearings, triangulating on three points: Catbrier Lane, Horse Hole on the Spanish Heights, and the Port Authority Dock. She couldn't count on her GPS. This hurricane had changed the course of Elijah's Creek. The configuration of the intersection was the same, but she couldn't find the street signs. She recognized the dogleg where the Red Dot Store and the gas station were supposed to be. Depot Road cut right, but there was no depot at the end. There was no post office down Post Office Road anymore either.

Six streets made up Elijah's Landing, counting Catbrier Lane and the dirt tracks that led to old Mr. Wallace's pig farm. The defunct rice paddy where the alligator and the Alligator Lady lived was pretty much filled in. There was a traffic light. It wasn't working on account of the storm.

The boy blue-tarping the roof of the old house shouted, "Hey! Here's a trunk. You want it while I'm up here?" Showing off for the girls, he lifted the trunk to his chest and braced it on the exposed cross beam. Sissy recognized it as a small, overseas packing crate. At some point, her dad had put hinges and a big padlock on it.

"Treasure!" a girl yelled. The next thing Sissy knew the trunk tumbled and all hands were scattering.

"Oops. My bad," said the kid on the roof.

They soon had the crate opened, taking a screwdriver to the hinges. It was full of her mother's books and scrapbooks. Sissy laid out the pages to dry on the picnic table, but she knew they were ruined. Tucked in an envelope and double-wrapped in tin foil were three photos labeled "Hurricane Gracie What's Left." Sissy knew them immediately. They were the three *Hurricane Sisters,* dated from just after WWII or the early fifties, little three-by-fours, black-and white with deckled edges.

Mozelle Geech Seabrook was the last to die. She was the one who got the best sendoff too—two cop cars, a motorcycle, and a fire truck. It had to have been small satisfaction since no sister was left to comment. All of them had died less than a year apart, but none of them ever became a storm statistic, despite the years of prediction and preparation.

Sissy remembered the motorcycle had seemed odd at a funeral. But in the photo, there was a teenaged Mozelle astride a Harley, hugging a young Marine and mugging for the camera. She wore a long-sleeved man's shirt, a perky scarf, and short-shorts.

Mozelle had been twelve when the Japanese bombed Pearl Harbor. She didn't have a sweetheart to write, but she greeted a lot of Marines at the Depot Train Station. One of them was Gunny. He missed the Big One but got into the fighting during Korea and three tours in Vietnam before he was killed.

Sissy could date her mother's photo almost to the month. Sissy was born in November of 1946. And there were her parents pictured at her father's duty station in Hawaii after the war. Her mother, wearing a lei and a muumuu, was about six months along. Rose Ida Tisdale vamped on the backseat of a white convertible. It was the black bathing suit that was a scandal. Later, bikinis and big cars were her trademark. She got away with speeding until Judge Ferguson revoked her license for driving 65 mph, the wrong way, down Elijah's Landing Road.

Sissy grinned remembering the friendship of these three women. Nothing in Sissy's experience could duplicate the bond between them.

She entered the house. The tarp gave her a sense of enclosure even though she could smell the mold growing on the wet Sheetrock and the carpet. She wandered to the back of the house, where the roof damage was less severe. The bathroom was nearly untouched.

Sissy tried the tap, forgetting the water was still turned off to prevent saltwater intrusion into the water supply. When she turned around she saw it: the hurricane tracking map.

She laughed.

The first requirement of a Hurricane Sister was to track the storms. Like a poodle dog, *sisters* kept one ear cocked to the latest advisory and the other to the latest gossip. They could clear a room of *come-heres* and snowbirds in gated communities and retirement villages by politely inquiring about hurricane tie-downs and flood insurance. They had hell-or-high-water bags packed and axes in the attic. The Hurricane Sisters had survived Gracie.

If there were a check list, Sissy knew she had every box ticked off. So, after rummaging in her purse for a pencil, she put a big X on the dot on the map for Elijah's Landing. She wrote *Sissy* next to it. Sissy'd come home.

Photo by Marge Boyle

THE EYE OF THE STORM

SEPTEMBER 1959
GRACIE

Rose Ida Tisdale would have slept until noon if Mrs. Forester had not checked each morning to see if the paper had been retrieved and the blinds opened. Catbrier Lane was a yes-sir, no-sir kind of neighborhood. Everybody operated on military time. Everybody understood o'dark thirty, except Rose Ida Tisdale.

Mrs. Forester discovered if she stood tiptoe in the bathtub and peered out the window, she could see Rose Ida's front door. Sometimes she sent Sissy or J. T. over. Most mornings, she phoned. "Are you up, Rose?" she said that September morning. "I think we have ourselves a hurricane."

The hurricane was Gracie. The weatherman brought Mrs. Forester's attention to the tropical storm on September 20, 1959. In her nine o'clock phone conference with Rose Ida, Mrs. Forester reported, "Don't worry yet, Rose. The steering currents are weak."

Mrs. Forester always called Rose Ida just Rose. She thought Rose Ida too Southern. It offended her Puritan streak. Of course, J. T. and Sissy didn't call her Rose Ida, either. At least, not around grownups. They always said Mrs. Tisdale. Secretly, they whispered, *That wild Rose Ida*.

J. T. got paddled for asking, "How come Mrs. Tisdale has a husband if she is *dee-vorced*?" It was Sissy who egged him—no, dared him—to ask.

7

Pushing her luck, Sissy also got him to inquire about *the three sheets to the wind*. Mrs. Forester went for the flyswatter over that.

Saturday, Rose Ida called early. "We've got to go shopping. I'm out of Co'-Cola."

"J. T. will run up to the station," Mrs. Forester answered. Rose Ida was having none of it. She was in a hurry. The stores closed on Saturday and Wednesday afternoons.

Mrs. Forester disapproved. For a minute, Sissy and J. T. thought they were going to be left behind. J. T. grinned his *I-know-what-I'm-going-to-get-into* grin, and Mrs. Forester relented. Since Mr. Forester had the duty, they all piled in Rose Ida's Caddy.

Riding with Rose Ida was always an adventure, because at any moment a parade might break out. She wore a white dress with black polka dots and a wide red sash. She put the car's top down and her sunglasses on. Sure enough, Rose Ida had to brake to parade speed as the vegetable man's mule and wagon pulled out from Elijah's Landing Road. Cars backed up behind them. J. T. stood up on the backseat and hollered at oncoming folks. They poked along until they got to the hospital. Mr. Leroy turned back toward the docks and the crab factory. Rose Ida waved and lit a cigarette before she sped off.

The A&P on the corner of Charles and Craven bustled with shoppers. There wasn't a parking place to be found. Rose Ida swooped around the corner. She found a spot near the old house where they plotted secession.

"You stay in the car, children," Mrs. Forester said. "No talking to strangers, locals, or Marines," she warned.

Rose Ida checked her makeup and tossed her head. "Be good now. I'll bring you a cold Co'-Cola."

In the time it took for J. T. to get bored with inspecting his toes, the vegetable man appeared. Customers leaving the grocery store crossed to check his offerings until the store manager came out, hands on his hips.

Mr. Leroy, the vegetable man, waved away the last housewife and hauled a bucket of water from the back of the wagon. He put it on the pavement with a grunt and then wiped his brow with a red do-rag.

J. T. climbed out of the Caddy and slouched over, his hands in his pockets. "What are you doing?"

Mr. Leroy told him, "Waterin' Ole Bad News, my mule."

"Can I help?"

"Go on … I said *git*. Yo' momma's callin'"

"She in the store. That's my sister," J. T. said.

Mr. Leroy groaned as he lifted the bucket. Ole Bad News shifted position, and the wagon rolled forward. Mr. Leroy dropped the bucket, with a sharp cry.

J. T. said, "What's the matter? You sick or something?"

"Whoa up, you. Lumbago and Ole Bad News. They goin' to have a storm. You heard that, son?"

"Yes, Mr. Leroy. I heard. Let me help you." The boy grabbed the bucket. He hoisted it, bracing it against his hip. The mule ducked its head in for a long drink and then rested its chin on the boy's shoulder.

Mr. Leroy chuckled and scratched the mule's ear. "Mmm. Hey, I thank you, son; but that there sister of yours be havin' a *fit*."

"Oh, her. Girls are like that."

The mule took a nip out of the boy's shoulder, leaving mule slobber on his striped T-shirt, dribbling down the front.

Mr. Leroy said, "Ole Bad News like you. What's your name?" The vegetable man took out his Buck knife and cut a length of sugar cane from his cart.

"My momma calls me Little Man except when she's mad. Now hah! You don't want to go getting her mad."

Mr. Leroy offered the sugar cane to him. "Is your momma the one with the red lipstick or the one with the red hair?"

"Red hair. You know my momma?"

"Oh, I seen her. What does your daddy call you?"

"Daddy calls me by my real name. J. T. It's J. T. Forester."

"Pleased to meet you, J. T. Forester. And the other lady?"

"That's Mrs. Tisdale."

Sissy came up, "John Thomas Forester, Momma says you git back to the car."

Mrs. Forester was waving. Rose Ida carried a carton of Coca-Cola and a bottle of bleach under her arms like white piglets. Behind her came the store manager with the rest of the groceries. The deputy sheriff's car pulled around the corner.

Mr. Leroy climbed into the wagon. "Time to go, Mr. J. T. Forester. Hand me that bucket. You watch out."

"Watch out for what?"

"Oh, you watch the clouds, and you'll see. Feels just like …oh, when was it? Nineteen thirty-nine or maybe forty. Got to watch out for the *nines*. Git up now. Ole Bad News, got some bad news. Git up!"

"Wait," Rose Ida called. "You got any shrimp?"

Mr. Leroy said, "No, missus. Not today."

"You git some shrimp, now. Come down Catbrier Lane to my house first," Rose Ida told him. "You know where I am?"

"Yes, missus. I know." He whistled to the mule and snapped the reins. "Ole Bad News, walk up."

"Nasty man," Rose Ida muttered as she climbed into the convertible.

Mrs. Forester commenced her lecture. She started with Little Man, progressed to J. T. and concluded, "John Thomas Forester. Just wait until your father gets home."

Rose Ida didn't answer the phone on Sunday morning. Mrs. Forester hustled the children into their church clothes and prodded them all out to the car. Mr. Forester fiddled with the car radio to tune in the local station as he backed out of the driveway, causing Mrs. Forester to get quite sharp with him and forget to look to see if Rose Ida's car was in front of her place.

After church, Mrs. Forester sent J. T. over to check on Rose Ida, who sent him down to the gas station for cigarettes and cola. Mrs. Forester spent the afternoon directing Mr. Forester and the children as they cleaned up the yard and stowed the outdoor furniture. Over Mr. Forester's protests, they boarded up the picture window in the front room.

It was a tad warm, and Rose Ida was sunbathing in her front yard.

"The nerve of that woman," Mrs. Forester told the contents of her freezer. She sighed and took out a couple of chickens to thaw. She filled empty milk cartons with water and packed them in the freezer. Then she patted the top as she closed the lid. That deep-dive freezer was her pride and joy.

Monday afternoon, Mr. Leroy the vegetable man came up the alley. Mrs. Forester was embarrassed to be caught scrubbing out her trashcan. She wiped her hands on her apron. "I don't need anything today."

"Evenin', missus. I knowed that, but the other lady, well, ah, she said if I got some shrimps to come down the lane to her first. They be fair jumpin' into the net. But the lady don't open the door," Mr. Leroy said.

Mrs. Forester looked down and twisted the corners of the apron. "Oh well, that's her way. I'll call her on the phone or send one of the kids over. That be all right?"

"Yes, missus."

"J. T.!" she called. Then to Mr. Leroy she said, "You do know there is a storm expected?"

"Sure do. Sherriff came out and told the folks to leave the Island tonight. Worried about the tides."

"And you have some place to shelter?" asked Mrs. Forester.

"Ole Bad News and me going to bed down in Mr. Wallace's barn. Have us some shrimps and a good rest."

"J. T.!" she called again. "Where is that boy? You go along to Mrs. Tisdale's. J. T. will be around. She'll open up for J. T."

"I thank you. Good evenin'."

Mrs. Forester called him back. "Mr. Leroy, aren't you worried?"

"No'm. Ole Bad News ain't worried neither. Don't you worry about your little brick house. Them builders done chopped down all the big trees," he chuckled. "Except for that ole pine. Them pines, they, well, ah …," he stopped, watching her anxious expression. "Don't take on so. You be fine," he said gently.

J. T. met Mr. Leroy in front of Rose Ida's. "Mrs. Tisdale wants to know if you got any cane juice," J. T. said. He handed the vegetable man money and a metal pail for the shrimp.

"Believe I do," Mr. Leroy said. "Believe I do." He filled the pail with ice and shrimp. Then he gave the boy two, pint canning jars wrapped in newspaper.

Monday evening, Mrs. Forester fried two chickens and boiled half a dozen eggs. She made her children take early baths and scrubbed the tub.

Then she filled it with water. She got Mr. Forester to bring the trash can into the kitchen and run the hose through the window. She filled the trash can and got down her big stockpot and rattled pans until Mr. Forester said, "Good Lord, woman. Come and sit down."

They watched the news.

Rose Ida called to say she was going to a hurricane party at the hospital. "The shelters are opening tonight so people will get to high ground. Aren't you coming?"

"No, we're going to ride it out here in our house. What about your house? Aren't you worried about your house?"

"No, honey. No place is safer than the firehouse, especially if you have your own fireman to serve you shrimp cocktails," Rose Ida said.

Mrs. Forester found it hard to sleep as her husband snored away. She padded through her house, checking on the children. She turned on the porch light and peered into the darkness. No sign of the storm. She pulled a sheet from the linen closet and wrapped up in it. She took a cautious step outside and sat on her back stoop, lighting a cigarette. The air felt heavy. Cigarette smoke wrapped around her shoulders like a shawl.

Toward morning, she fell asleep on the sofa, but awoke with a start to a milky gray morning. A spatter of rain hit the windows.

"It's not so bad," she said, as she put on a pot of coffee. She was able to feed her family a good breakfast. The lights went out at ten o-clock. By noon, the water was off.

Hurricane Gracie's wind sang in the wires and the trees, a low hum vibrating though the brick house on Catbrier Lane as Mrs. Forester served lunch. The family ate a picnic of fried chicken and Spam sandwiches in the dining room. "Drink up your milk," she told her children. "It will spoil."

Water dripped from the overhead light fixture—first a spatter and then a determined tinkling as Mrs. Forester placed china bowls and cups to catch the water. The indoor picnic turned to panic, and she rushed to find a bucket.

As the barometric pressure fell, the song of the storm swelled to a roar rattling the picture window till a crack appeared like a vein. The house dug in to fight the winds, shuddering in place, but the roof of the shed peeled right back. The tall pine in back shoved up the sandy soil as it leaned away from the house. "We're going to be okay," she said.

The eye of the storm brought silence for thirty minutes; then the wind returned. The house shook all over. The pine tree leaned in the opposite direction. Debris slammed into the back of the house, shattering the big bedroom window. Mr. Forester hastily moved their double mattress into the living room where Mrs. Forester made up the bed. She and Sissy cowered, arms around each other. She could feel the storm in her brain, like the lightning of a migraine, deep tissues and muscles throbbing to the beat of her heart. She covered her ears to the roar of the storm.

Mr. Forester pushed the sofa against the front door. "Holy shit, Kate! Holy shit," he said, watching shingles and siding fly.

"There goes the shed!" J. T. said.

"Get away from that window!" Mrs. Forester called. She wouldn't look. She ducked under the sheet around her shoulders. "Language, Ted. The children," she told him.

Her husband came and sat on the floor beside her. "Come here, J. T.," he said, and then to her, "We should have gone to the shelter."

They huddled for two lifetimes. The neighborhood flying around and into the house as they waited it out. Finally, the clatter and roar diminished. Exhausted, Mrs. Forester fell asleep.

*   *   *

Rose Ida was calling. "Yoo hoo! I'm back. We survived Gracie." The sound of a chain saw punctuated her chatter. "We got the grills going. What have you got in your freezer to fill the pot? How about Frogmore Stew? I've got the shrimp. I'm making sweet cane tea, no ice though," Rose Ida rummaged through Mrs. Forester's freezer.

"Keep the freezer closed," Mrs. Forester said. She refused to get up from her mattress on the living room floor. She pulled the sheet over her head. "Keep the cold in."

Rose Ida laughed carelessly. "Kate, hon, the lights are going to be out for days. We got to eat this up. No use letting food spoil. Let's see, corn, tomatoes … What's this? Venison sausage. Wow. I'm taking your stock pot. We've got a mess of folks to feed," she said.

Still, Kate Forester refused to move from the mattress. The screen door slammed. Someone tip-toed in and then out, slamming the door again. She could hear Rose Ida laughing. The door slammed a third time. Kate sat up. "Don't slam the door," she called automatically. The sound of the saw began again. A streak of sunlight worked its way through cracks in the boarded-up front window.

Kate got up and opened the back door. She couldn't recognize her yard. It was a circus. The whole neighborhood had arrived for dinner. Aubrey Tisdale, Rose Ida's new husband, man-handled the fallen branches into a pile and doused them with gasoline. A bonfire whooshed to life to cheers and clapping. Rose Ida, ringmaster, presided over the grills. She handed out beers to a group of young Marines, jar-headed and fine.

Leroy Blue rode his mule down the alley and picked his way through the debris. "Good evenin', missus," he called to her when he noticed her at the screen door. "Ole Bad News got some good news: All's well. The good Lord suffered nary a hair on man, mule, or pig be harmed. Though Mr. Wallace can't promise the pig nothin'."

Rose Ida said, "What about the folks on the Island?"

"As soon as I can ride this here mule across the bridge, I aim to find out," Mr. Leroy said. "Weren't I right, missus?"

Kate looked at the hole in the roof of her brick house for the first time and began to cry.

"Hush, missus. This here storm weren't anythin'. My uncle John, he say that. He be a boy when the big one come. This girl, Gracie. Shoot, she's just a squall."

Mr. Forester and Aubrey Tisdale pried plywood from the front window with a screech of nails. Two firemen, looking like circus clowns in their turn-out gear, maneuvered the panel over the hole in the roof and nailed it down. They tented the roof with a tarp and climbed down.

"Y'all head over to my house, next," Rose Ida yelled. "Come on, Kate, hon. What you need is some of Mr. Leroy's sweet cane tea," she said. She handed Mrs. Forester a glass of strong, dark liquid. "Right, Mr. Leroy?"

"Won't hurt none. Got to scat on over the Island before the deputy makes his rounds. No tellin' what the man goin' to find."

Rose Ida waved him on with a laugh. She lit a cigarette.

Kate turned on her with a fury matching her red hair. "How can you laugh? Look, look at my house. Your house. This mess. You'd think you were at a carnival."

"You just stop. Kate, hon; you can't even throw a convincing hissy fit," Rose Ida said. "It's not the end of days. That house is just full of stuff the movers didn't lose. How many times have you moved since Ted came home from the Pacific? How many pairs of curtains have you just left hanging in your quarters?" She blew a smoke ring. "Look at your Ted, my Aubrey. They are fine. J. T. and Sissy. Everything is going to be all right."

Kate continued to cry, but she drank the tea and pushed her red hair out of her eyes. She sniffed. "What's in this?"

Rose Ida sat on the back stoop. She took a puff and offered her cigarette to Kate. The end smeared with lipstick.

Kate shook her head. "You put on makeup for the hurricane?" she asked in disbelief. "I bet you would powder your nose for Judgment Day."

Rose Ida put her arm around Kate. "I'll tell you what the day of wrath is like: when I waited to die." She sighed and continued. "Now, you know my ex-husband not a mean man. He just buttoned down and starched up. Pole up his ass, you know what I mean? The guy gets leave, discovers his little woman has taken a job. Uh huh." She took a drag on the cigarette and blew a smoke kiss.

She sat up straight. "*His little woman,*" she snorted. "How was I to know the job in the base laundry was 'conduct unbecoming'? All those boys needed clean drawers. Summer whites and caps; Jesus, Mary, and Joseph, every one of those mothers' sons went to war with clean underwear. What is so bad about bleach?"

Kate nodded.

"I left him. *Aubrey* appreciates me. He knows I still iron a mean pleat," Rose Ida said.

Kate knew there was more to it. "What did you do?" she asked.

"Well, for starters, I put white glue in the rinse instead of starch."

Kate smiled for the first time. "I heard your ex-husband was a stand-up kind of guy," she said softly.

Rose Ida whooped and spilled her sweet cane tea. "Sister Kate, you got that right. You just got to give life a pat and a promise. Want some more of Leroy Blue's tea?"

"No, Sister Rose. I believe a Co'-Cola would be fine."

"Steaks are ready and coffee is up," yelled the men around the fire. Ted Forester came over with a cup in his hand. He hesitated. "Kate, honey," he said. "Do we have any milk for the coffee?"

He saw her expression. "That's all right. Never mind. We'll drink it black."

Kate went inside her little brick house. She opened her freezer and grabbed an ice cream carton. She gave that freezer a pat and a promise to drain the overflowing drip pan. She put two tablespoons of vanilla in her husband's coffee. When her sleepyheads got up the next morning, she served a breakfast of cereal and melted ice cream sundaes with canned peaches.

Photo by Marge Boyle

HAINT BLUE

'T'aint haints 'sactly
but a pileated woodpecker,
great buster of a bird,
tap, tap, tapping on my sills and fascia.
Not eating the cedar clapboards 'sactly
but feasting on the creamy grubs
of black bottomed bees.
Mr. Leroy, he say,
"Slap up a coat of paint."
Which be why
mine is the house with
blue sills and door posts.
Can't hurt.

Photo by Marge Boyle

BOY IN A STORM

———————◦◦◦◦———————

AUGUST 1, 1964

Plum-like in the tree above him, twelve year old Prudence Seabrook watched the pale movements of her cousin's head and hand. She dropped twigs and launched shreds of moss and bark. Grimly, he continued writing, never acknowledging the torment or the tormentor. He steeled himself not to start when a missile creased his ear and landed on his notebook.

The pleasure of her game soon died. She surveyed the upper reaches of the oak. A vagrant breeze stirred the branches and caused a strand of Spanish moss to brush her lips. She snatched the offending graybeard and rolled it into a tangle. She let the moss fall. It landed wig-like on his head.

"Connie boy," she called to him despite the fact he was eight years her senior. Prudence was the half of the Seabrook twins who thought everyone should have a sitting tree. Her sister, Patience, preferred sitting under trees and making goo-goo eyes at their cousin, Conway Eustis.

Conway—or Connie boy, as the twins dubbed him—retrieved the moss and threw it back. It fell short. Prudence laughed and climbed higher.

"What?" she asked far above him, closer to the truth of the day than he, with a plum-proud heart, deep and dark with a changeling's wisdom. "What are you writin'?"

"A song," he said. "A poem."

Connie called himself a poet. He would write a play seamed with Southern color and the creak of the blackbird. He spent his evenings lounging on the front porch, feeling the sun set, the paint crumble, and the wisteria bloom. He scrabbled down the night. He listened to the neighbors talk, in the hope that someone would repeat the guarded charm, the incantation that would transmute life into the blue truth and truth into the written word.

Prudence and Patience, who knew the spell, laughed and teased him. The family, like Caesar's Gaul, was divided into three parts: the Geeches, who were the shrimpers; the Seabrooks, all good little Marines; and the Eustis cousins, who were useless. The twins mocked the notebooks he kept.

He filled them with every thought that crossed his path. He transcribed supper on a paper napkin. With all manner of hieroglyphics, he preserved dialect, tone, and ambiance. He hurried from the table to preserve the dialogue before it slipped away.

Prudence laughed. She talked endlessly and spilled out the furnishings of her mind, showing him the contents of a pocket, telling him the tales a child tells a younger one. He was suffused with wonder. He recorded the gossip and legends of childhood.

She sat in the June night with the knobs of her backbone braced on the lip of the second step. Her legs ranged down the remaining step so that she could pinch the blades of grass between her toes.

"And the snake stretched nearly all the way across this porch," Prudence said. "Big. Big around as this." Prudence wrapped her arms around the column that supported the porch roof.

Patience nodded affirmation. She took up the story. "Poor Clara's eyes got big and black and round. She let out such a screech that Grandpop came running from the boatyard. His glasses popped off his face. He stepped on them!"

Prudence did the sound effects and quoted their grandfather, Tillis Geech. "'In God's name,' he said. 'In God's name.' Grandpop took up the fallen broom and slashed the empty air."

Prudence gulped for air and relished Connie's discomfort. "Right there," she pointed. "It was right there. Then it slid off the porch without so much as a by-your-leave. I bet it's still there, right underneath that porch."

Connie shifted his position, opened his notebook, and picked up his pen in cold horror. Patience batted her eyes sweetly.

The twins remembered the day he arrived on the train with his books. He came, newly educated—or at least newly graduated—to spend the summer. He had come to write and to think. He had a graduate-teaching assistantship starting in the middle of August. He said he would be no trouble and offered to pay his room and board.

"To pay?" Grandpop laughed. "With what?"

In words, Prudence guessed, or in books, or in truth if he could find it.

Connie had tripped as he stepped down from the station platform, spilling an armload of books. The porter behind him chuckled and gathered up the fluttering crop of paperbacks. Once the books were harvested, Connie tipped the man and leaned over to pick up his bags. He found them too heavy and left them. He came to meet his relatives uncertainly, hand outstretched, pale, skinny, and sweat-stained.

"A boy," said their grandmother.

"A damned fool," their grandpop said.

But he had all those books. Prudence devoured them. He bribed her with some to gossip. He plied her with harmless novels, yellow-bound westerns and bloodless mysteries. They prowled the township library looking for other books and newspapers.

She was more interested in the books he would not give up. She read while he was not looking, skimming swiftly the pages he left open, the underlined portions that fell under her gaze. After a while, when he trusted her, she read his notebooks. Sometimes he read his work to her, ignoring her giggles, often enthralling her.

He sought the back issues of the local paper. He read aloud from the legal notices, obituaries, wedding announcements, the names and towns in a low monotone. He mouthed the words like a new reader in order to understand them.

"The families of the late ..." he read one yellowed page and wrote on another just for the assonance and the nonsense of it.

"William Grieves
and unknown heirs at law
next of kin and distributees
of said William Grieves.
If deceased
Lurretia Grieves
and unknown heirs at law
next of kin and distributees
of said Lurretia Grieves.
If deceased …"

Prudence and Patience listened to the sing-song for a moment and then yawned twin signals of boredom. Connie stopped reading out loud but continued writing names.

"Sadly missed by family and friends, Alice Blue."

He turned to one drowsy girl. It was Prudence, perhaps.

"Who is Alice Blue?" Connie asked.

"A witch," said Patience.

A root woman," said Prudence not missing a beat, so it sounded as if only one of them had answered.

He stared at Prudence. She sat, hands folded on the page she was reading as if sitting for a portrait. He wrote, trying to conceal his inner excitement: "Alice Blue—Witch—Research."

He questioned Prudence and Patience carefully, knowing too much interest would put them on guard. "Witch? Why do you say that?"

"Alice Blue was a witch. A root woman," Prudence whispered. She put her finger to her lips. "Sh," she said. "We have to go home."

Connie thumbed the earlier editions of the paper until he found the stark black notice of death. He noted the facts:

Alice Blue/Died April 5, 1958
Said to be 104
Survived by one son, two daughters, seven grandchildren, five great-grandchildren and two great-great-grandchildren.

Connie looked at the words he had written. Patterns grew, and a portrait formed. Finally, he wrote on another page his own fiction.

Alice Blue had ten children of whom only three did not precede her in death. Her exact date of birth is unknown. The original record in the ledger of Rutledge Eustis, her father's master (burned in the great fire of 1867), ran as follows: "daughter to Truman and Col. Lawson's Gracie. Child and mother bought this day, Aug. 5, 1854. Alice married in 1871 to Walker Blue tenant farmer. Walker died in 1893, the year of the great storm."

His hands trembled in the haste to record his whirling thoughts. He gathered up his things and went into the humid afternoon, setting for himself a panting pace. His thoughts were running far ahead down the still-hot side streets.

Prudence was stripping the bark from a sassafras sapling. Her short, dark hair was slicked to her head. Patience, ladylike in the porch rocker, shelled butterbeans. Connie ranged on the steps feeling no urge to enter the house. He sat very still in order to preserve the cloying nearness of the hour.

The maid came to the door and opened the screen to let the dog out. She let it bang shut. Behind them in the kitchen, she sang a tuneless refrain. Prudence looked up, twitching the tip of the stick toward the house. "Our maid Clara's grandma," she said.

"What?"

"Her grandma was the root woman."

The maid's voice rose darkly in song. Her words were not recognizable.

*   *   *

August 2, 1964

"There are lots of Snipes here," Prudence said, one steaming August afternoon. Beneath a dense canopy of funereal moss, they stood swatting mosquitoes.

"Lots," Patience echoed.

The graves were marked by the withered skull-like forms of conch shells. The brooding of the half-tended, half-forgotten dead filled Connie with anticipatory dread. He read the headstone. "Blackshear Snipe 1891–1958."

This was the burying ground of the colored Snipes, Jenkinses, and Smalls. Contained in the fenced plot were the departed kin of slaves and freemen. New mounds appeared as if thrust up from inside the earth. They were marked, dated, and mourned in a dreadful hurry and were left to meditate under the eternal curtain of the graybeard moss.

Connie reached out to touch one stone. He probed the carving of a stylized flower above the name. She who was buried there had been called Dessie.

"I used to be afraid to come here," Prudence said. "I saw faces in the moss. *Them*."

A spider crawled across the face of the stone. Connie drew back as if bitten. The air had become hotly still and oppressive. Suddenly a jay flew up squawking. Connie started again, dropping his pen.

"Just a blue jay," Patience said.

Just a blue omen, he thought.

Together, they scratched in the leaves for the pen. Far above, the unseen sky purpled with thunderheads, and the tree-dim cemetery darkened.

Connie, on his knees, turned pen in hand to one tiny grave labeled *Infant Boy*. It was graced by a blond Madonna in a blue, painted crate.

"Blond Mary, brown baby, blue crate," Connie wrote in his notebook.

"Blue," Prudence said as he wrote the word, "is a *good* color. The evil spirits can't cross it. That's why they paint the shutters and doors blue."

Patience continued in a hushed voice, "To keep the ghosts away. No paint on the wall, only the blue doors and windows. The wind may blow through, but evil may not pass."

Prudence laughed, and her laughter was echoed by the thunder. Connie did not hear her. He copied the words from the grave, not what the thunder said. He tucked the pen into his pocket and snapped the notebook shut.

He hurried from the mossy gloom to the road where the sunlight still fragmented upon the yellow sand. The girls' laughter followed him as the first drops of rain darkened the sun stains.

August 3, 1964

Then the dog days of August were upon them, with the humidity arousing in them a kind of hydrophobic madness, the imperious insanity of old Caesar's month. The twins supposed that was why Grandpop had even considered the absurd suggestion. Connie proposed it. Grandpop acted upon it. It was done before the thunderclouds of the next day's four o'clock shower had piled anvil-like over the bay.

"Is there an island?" Connie began tentatively. He chose the most inopportune moment after dinner, just as the warm red-hearted melon of a sun began to set and before Grandpop Geech and his brother, Grady, had finished their cigarettes properly. Tillis and Grady Geech exchanged identical wolfish grins.

"Island? This whole damn island is an island," Grandpop answered.

"I know," said Connie with sophomoric seriousness. "I mean an unsettled one. You know, with just a few tenant farmers. One with no bridge—cut off ...."

"An 'unsettled' island?" Grandpop repeated. His eyes met Grady Geech's deep blue ones. The Geech brothers flickered smiles of acknowledgment. They knew the place, a place for outcasts, mosquitoes, and lonesome goats.

"Where I can go to sort of camp out?" Connie continued.

"Camp out?" echoed Grandpop as if he were hearing impaired.

"To talk to the people. Study their dialect. Ask questions."

"Aren't there enough people on this island?" asked the twins' mother, clattering the silver and the china as she cleared.

"I want the true dialect of the Negroes, Aunt Mozelle," he said.

"Go on out to the kitchen. Talk to Clara, our maid," Grady Geech instructed. "Go see Ben, whose arm Dr. Otis sewed back on. Or chat with the good doctor himself. Julian's heart is white, but his tongue can render the Gullah like a nigger."

Grandpop laughed and crushed out the cigarette in the mashed potatoes. Mozelle Seabrook frowned at the gesture but held her tongue in deference to the irrationality of August.

"The dialect," Connie said again.

"Hunger," interrupted Grady. "Study the hunger. The poverty. The disease. But the dialect?" He made an elegant but meaningless gesture.

"Now, Uncle Grady, don't get on your soapbox tonight," chided Mozelle, returning from the kitchen. As the swinging door closed, they caught a breath of the maid's dark toneless song.

"Oh, oh sweet Jesus," she sang.

"Save your speech for Washington when Fritz calls," Mozelle finished.

They discussed election politics. In a pause in the debate, Connie inserted his request again. He was so mirthlessly earnest. When he insisted, they made plans with exaggerated tolerance.

Grandpop and Grady Geech took him over the next day, crossing the expanse of brackish water in the shrimp boat, *Sweet Mozelle*. Amidships, Connie rocked with a greenish cast around his mouth as Grady steered deliberately across the wake of a larger, homecoming trawler. The small boat thumped and bumped its way toward the barrier island crowned with live oak, slash and loblolly pine. They left him on a strip of sandbar to wade with his tent and supplies the hundred feet to the shore. They waited and were rewarded to see him stumble, fall, and rise from the shallows like Neptune, streaming.

"At least he's not tryin' to register them to vote," said Grandpop as curious goats appeared at the edge of the woods. "Were we ever like that, Grady? Willing to leave everything behind? Go somewhere, anywhere to get shut of home and the old lady and listen to stories?"

August 4, 1964

The next afternoon had gone all green; even the wisteria coveted the air. The day held its breath for the onset of a squall. A tropical storm watch had been posted. Prudence paced the length of the porch, the hairs on her arms rising with the building static charge. Patience was parked beneath the fan in the front room, too ladylike to do more than glow in the afternoon heat.

Clara Blue, the maid, came out. She sat in the yellow rocker. My, my," she said, fanning herself with a funeral home paddle fan. "My, my."

Prudence did another turn around the porch and threw herself down at the black woman's feet.

"Mighty quiet, girl," Clara commented.

"Nothin' to do." Prudence stretched out on the wooden boards and clasped her hands behind her head. "Would you tell me somethin'?" she asked.

"If'n I can."

"Tell me about your grandma and the old times."

"My, my, child. You're soundin' like Mr. Connie."

"Him," Prudence snorted. "He doesn't know anythin'."

The thunder rumbled as if in concurrence. Prudence rolled over as Clara peered at the leaden sky. "Old man's rollin' them watermelons," she observed.

"Do you remember any spells?" Prudence asked.

"No, thank you, Jesus. No, girl!"

Prudence lay with her chin on her fists. A shiver of wind lifted the multileafed wisteria. Prudence shook as if she were also part of the plant, a trembling leaf. The maid rocked on, thumping the porch with her wide flat feet.

"Did you ever see her work a spell?"

Half asleep, she opened one eye and looked the girl over. "Where do you get such questions?"

"Did you?" Prudence waited.

"Once," she began. "I 'member that old man, Blackshear. That old man, he have the fallin' out sickness. It come on him sudden like. All at once he be fallin' on the floor, eyes gone back, a-twitchin'.

His daughter be Dessie. She love that old man, love him more than Tom, her own man. Or the baby she goin' have. She *love* her papa. Take care of him like a baby."

Lightning illuminated the purple clouds over the bay. Prudence rose to her feet, counting. The thunder grumbled around them, cautioning them not to meddle. The maid rocked back and forth, thumping, the rhythm slowing. "Ain't no story for a child like you," she murmured.

"I'm almost thirteen."

Clara leaned back holding herself rigid. She closed her eyes. "Praise Jesus."

Prudence made herself small. Lightning flashed again. The treetops began to sway. For a moment, Prudence wondered where her cousin was and how he would fare in the storm. With a smile, she imagined how disappointed he would be when he found out that she had *scooped* him.

Presently, the maid continued in a lower voice. "Old Black, he fall out on the tracks one day. His head split open. He dead."

She stopped.

Prudence knew better than to prompt her. She sat hugging her knees.

Clara continued, "They carry him up to Dessie's house. She go on like crazy. Her Tom couldn't hold her. He afraid she lose her baby, she screechin' so. She vow no man would take her pa and put dirt on his face. She lock Tom out." Raindrops began to spot the porch steps like Dessie's tears.

Prudence kept her eye on the leading edge of the precipitation. "And?" she asked when the woman seemed to have forgotten to tell the story out loud.

"And they send for Granny. She an old lady, past a hundred. She call, 'Dessie?' And Dessie say, 'No one goin' to put dirt in my pa's face.'

Granny, she call out, 'Dessie!'

Dessie open the door a crack. 'I come to see Blackshear Snipe. He here?' She say, 'He here.'

And she shut the door quicker than blackbird flight. Granny *fram* the door. 'Dessie,' she call. 'Open the door!'"

Clara paused and then continued, "Dessie know that voice, the sound of the root woman. Nobody cross Granny when she use that voice. Dessie open the door. Granny say, 'Give me yo hand.'

"Dessie hold out her hand. Granny grip it hard and tie blue yarn around her finger."

Clara stopped and held up her own dark hand to show Prudence how it done. Prudence held up her hand in imitation. Clara gripped it. She continued in a deep, sleepy voice. "'Where be yo Pa?' Granny ask Dessie. Dessie show her the old man, dark and bloody."

Prudence gasped. Clara drew the girl toward her, upward until Prudence knelt with her elbows on the black woman's ample knees. The woman grasped Prudence's other wrist, pulling her even closer.

"The others crowd in round the body," Clara whispered, her breath warm on Prudence's face.

"Granny took his hand and tied the other end of the yarn round his finger. There they be, Dessie and Black, join to each other. Granny sing out for the kitchen shears. Some them folks standin' by go off to tell the preacher. Others, they just watch. Granny say, soft, low 'Across the blue, no evil passes'. She cut the yarn a'bindin' the two, separate Dessie from death."

Clara clapped Prudence's hands together. Prudence slid to the floor, breathless. She rolled away from Clara to the edge of the porch where the rain cooled her face.

"What happened?" asked Prudence. Clara folded her hands and rocked back. Prudence shuddered and closed her eyes. She held her breath to hear the answer without distortion. She must savor the moment.

Finally, Clara said, "Dessie ... she let them put her pa in the ground and went home to have the baby. Baby die."

Silence strung tautly between them as Prudence tried to imagine Dessie's travail.

Like scissors, Clara's voice cut the air. "Dessie die." Another minute of stillness elapsed, enhanced by silence from the clouds. Clara rocked. "Granny die too." She began to sing.

Prudence shivered in the rain, filled with the simplicity of it. She had never considered death before. She watched a leaf as a drop of water formed, grew heavy, and fell earthward. She tried to hum the refrain, to seal it in her mind for her cousin Connie. "Across the blue, no evil passes"

"Here be your grandpop," Clara heaved herself out of the rocker as Tillis Geech came up the walk. The rain sputtered into steam. Prudence sat up and watched her grandpop shake off the moisture but not the fishy smell of his profession.

He looked his granddaughter over.

She was sure he would find some fault. She gave him the kiss of simpering innocence.

He gave her a curt nod. "Good evenin',"

"Good evenin'," she answered, with exaggerated civility. "Storm a'comin'."

"Storm's coming," Geech repeated, correcting his granddaughter's diction.

Then Prudence rolled her eyes and struck back with soft precision. "Wonder how Connie farin'," she said. It was a child's the presumption, guaranteed to set the seal of doom on dinner conversation, as if politics weren't enough.

* * *

The deluge came at dark as Grandpop and the twins sat in the living room, reading the convention headlines. He read aloud to his granddaughters with withering editorial comments.

Patience sat like a pupil at her lessons, nodding or frowning when prompted. On the floor, Prudence tried to read the discarded pages. She watched Grandpop out of the corner of her eye, wondering how she would grieve his sudden passing. Flashes of lightning lit up the window-side of his face with an unsettling glow. "Those poor boys," Prudence murmured in an attempt to stop the tirade. She looked up as Grandpop let the paper slide to the floor.

"What's that?" he asked grumpily.

"In Mississippi," she answered.

Prudence scanned the headlines and the distorted photos, her sister leaning over her shoulder. "That one looks like Connie boy," Patience said.

Prudence thought again of the rain and scrub-crowned island. She sought a pencil and paper.

Grandpop lit a cigarette and blew smoke rings into the lamplight. "Humph," he cleared his throat. "Those Jew boys don't know any better, but you'd think that the colored'un would have knowed his place."

Prudence realized that she was only scandalized by his deliberate use of poor grammar. She looked at the photos and at her grandfather's unyielding profile.

"Communists," he said. "They've gone underground."

Prudence read the names again. They were good names, like characters in a play, Schwerner, Goodman and Chaney. They were the kinds of names Connie recorded and tried to memorize. She copied them, shaping the letters as if in their very form they could reveal more than the literal content of their sound. Then she added a name of her own, *Blackshear Snipe*.

The phone rang. Grandpop cursed again as he stalked to answer it.

An unfamiliar voice questioned him with drowsy authority. "Well, sir," came the voice from the other side of the deluge. "This is Griffin, Chatham County Sheriff's Department. We have a little problem here. My men picked up this white boy out on Sandaw Island. Says he's your nephew. Looks real suspicious, no I.D. Askin' a lot of questions, makin' folks uneasy. Maybe one of them outside agitators. One of them missin' boys."

"What name does he give?"

"Conway Eustis."

"Damn it all. Let me speak to him."

He shouted into the receiver for a few minutes and slammed it down. In a whirl, he was away.

Later, Prudence and Patience watched for him to come back with Connie from the bedroom window as the evening darkened into the texture of molten pitch.

Prudence's fingers spread over the inside of the pane. She was alert to any small tremor that would reveal the drama of the event—any change, any sudden coolness that would allow her fingers to see more than her eyes. She pressed the thumb and finger of her left hand to her eyelids. Her blinded eyes strained to see past the self-imposed handicap. She saw only darkness. No trace of the watery world beyond the glass remained.

She looked deeper into herself, seeing only the kaleidoscopic blue of the closed eye.

"*Across the blue no evil passes,*" she recited. She got no response. Patience had fallen asleep. Lightning whitened the exterior landscape. There were no answers here. It was as if she had awakened from a dream that had stolen all her wisdom. She remembered laughing at Connie. Now she had forgotten the reason she had been so amused. "But it did. Evil came right over"

The headlights of the car snaked up the road and into the driveway. Grandpop hurried toward the house without a backward look at Connie boy's slender, soulful form standing alone by the car. Rain-streaked and miserable, his face was illuminated by the flashes of lightning. He looked toward his cousin's bedroom window.

Don't look to me, Prudence thought, suddenly angry. *It will come like a storm and some will fall.*

Patience stirred in her sleep, mumbling softly.

Prudence jumped to her bed. Bouncing to get some height, she leaped to her twin's bed.

"What? What is it?" cried Patience sitting up, clutching her sheet. "Is it a hurricane?"

A tremendous flash and crash of thunder shook the house. The sisters clung together.

"Nothing," Prudence said after a few seconds of catching her heart and her breath. "Some old boy out in the storm."

Photo by Marge Boyle

MARE'S TALES AND MACKEREL SKIES

Rose Ida Tisdale held court on the dock at Elijah's Landing, a royal of the raggle-taggle gypsies-o. She was the queen of misplaced objects and hopeless causes. She wanted to know "How in the world do you lose a shrimp boat, Mozelle?"

Mozelle Seabrook looked like Jackie Kennedy in her yellow shift with the white binding, perky kerchief, and sunglasses. She frowned. When she opened her mouth, the illusion was dispelled. "Y'all don't know my poor daddy. Mama say you look up 'lost,' it be Daddy grinnin' out the dictionary at you."

She gave a shivery sigh and smoothed her yellow shift. She peered seaward at the three boats on the horizon. "Daddy, Daddy. Just like him to set out in December and not show up until the next August. Where has he been?"

"Don't hardly know," said Rose Ida. "Sounds like a Geech to me."

Mozelle's father, Tillis, had taken out his shrimper, the *Sweet Mozelle*, a few days before Christmas saying he was going to fish for presents. He had disappeared. Not a trace of the man or his boat had been found. Her uncle Grady had never given up. Only the day before a Department of Natural Resources boat had spotted the *Sweet Mozelle* drifting abandoned and had contacted the family. Grady Geech and the Department of Natural Resources officer were towing the *Sweet Mozelle* home.

Kate Forester nodded sadly. Kate was the practical one. She waited on the dock in her practical jeans and her practical Keds. Her red hair was cut into a cap of curls with bangs like Mamie Eisenhower's. She said, "I bet there are no presents for you. You have to prepare yourself, Mozelle. It's been almost nine months. You might never find out what happened."

Rose Ida fanned herself with both hands and did a little dance with the rising wind, switching the little bit of skirt she wore. "You think that little boat's been driftin' all this time? I foretell your daddy's been squirreled up somewhere. Jacksonville. Miami." Rose Ida said.

Kate tried to change the subject. "Did you get the weather report on Camille this morning? The gulf's going to get hit hard."

"Better them than us. It's a year endin' in nine. I've heard of storms crossin' right over Florida and hittin' us on the backside," said Mozelle.

The trio scanned the sky for the telltale signs of any approaching storm. Folks said mare's tail cloud formations signaled a cold front, setting up the clash of atmospheres leading up to stormy weather. To the southeast, past Little Dog Key, a gray-green mackerel sky indicated a warm front moving in. The wind was wet and tropical.

Rose Ida recited,

"Mares tails and mackerel skies.
A gale she blows, prudence cries.
The striker knows to raise the net.
Prudence and patience ne're forget."

Mozelle said, "I see it. I'd recognize *Sweet Mozelle*'s blue stripe anywhere. Oh, Daddy, what has become of you?"

Tillis Geech's shrimp boat had been named for her. He had wanted to name the new boat when his first son was born. After six daughters, he decided not to wait any longer. If there was anybody who knew shrimp, it would be *those* Geech boys. If there was anybody who couldn't make a dollar, it was *that* Geech boy.

Mozelle continued, "The Department of Natural Resources Officer who found her drifting thinks she ran aground until Tropical Storm Anne floated her off."

"But all this time?" persisted Kate. "Where has your father been since Christmas? It doesn't make sense."

Rose Ida shushed her. "A Geech is a Geech. And show me a Geech who couldn't man a shrimp trawler by himself."

Well … the Geeches *weren't* always Geeches. The first one anybody heard of seems to have jumped ship and hid out on Little Dog Key long about 1870. He was a Greek with a name about fourteen syllables long—a fisherman whose family had probably been tending nets since before Homer. Mispronounced by the locals, the name shortened to Geech. It had been written "Geech" when the Quaker teacher lady counted noses, white and black, and then, up and married him.

The Department of Natural Resources boat tied up. The DNR officer was met by a sheriff's deputy, wearing his regulation badge and belly. Grady Geech maneuvered his trawler and the *Sweet Mozelle* with his two-man crew. The smell of diesel fuel was sooty. They could taste the oil on the wind.

As the small shrimp trawler bumped the dock, Rose Ida leaped impulsively to its deck, wobbling a little on her backless heels. She ducked into the cockpit, but backed out quickly with a despairing cry. "There is somebody down there," she yelled. She pointed a long quivering finger. "Y'all come out here. Your family's a-waitin' on you."

Mozelle joined her, clutching her hands to her chest. "Daddy? Is it my daddy?" She cried again and stumbled against Rose Ida. The two women turned to stare at rusty red stains on the deck.

"Oh Lordy," Rose Ida keened. "Oh my Lordy."

There was skittering and scratching from below. Two brown-skinned boys tumbled to the deck. They were filthy with matted black hair and wild eyes. There was no telling what color birthday suits they had. Dressed in dark cut-offs and nothing else, they smelled of fuel and all the little fishy and shrimpy things in the hold. "*Señora Mozelle. Señora Mozelle*," one of them cried. He held a crumpled photo of Tillis Geech and Mozelle for her to see. "*Por favor.*"

He tried to embrace her and succeeded in covering her shift with oily hand prints. The older of the two pulled him back with a torrent of Spanish. He looked up to see the deputy putting on some speed. He pushed his brother. "*Policía*," he said.

The pair broke like a covey of quail, running in opposite directions. The smaller boy ran to the stern and then jumped to the dock. The larger boy headed forward, leaped to Grady Geech's trawler. He sped the length of the shrimper before jumping from the boat. The boys pounded up the pier hitting the sands. One fell in the oyster bed and *pluff* mud but was pulled up, bleeding.

Kate Forester figured she got the situation under control in the next fifteen minutes. She dispatched Rose Ida home with palpitations. She staunched the boy's tears and bloody knees with her Canal Zone Spanish and a discreetly placed sanitary napkin. After informing the County's Finest how inadequate the first-aid kit from the deputy's patrol car was, and suggesting, *por favor,* the man follow her back to Catbrier Lane, she joined her Ted in the car. "What a ding dong awful mess," she told Ted. "You know what I think? Those little boys are from Cuba. Do you suppose Geech got mixed up with Fidel Castro?"

Ted allowed that he didn't know.

It was Kate who thought of J. T.'s Spanish teacher. The deputy rounded her up when he could not reach anyone from Social Services to take the boys in hand. Kate cleaned them up and dressed them in J. T.'s hand-me-downs. The older boy, about twelve or thirteen, she guessed but the other much younger, all baby fat and dimples.

Kate put on coffee and made tea, magically producing sticky buns to boot. Then she called a conference in the living room of her little brick house. The two boys sat nervously on the sofa with the Spanish teacher and Grady. Ted brought in kitchen chairs. Rose Ida and Aubrey showed up at the last minute, Rose Ida predicting a grand, gossip-rich scene too tasty to miss.

"This is *Señora* Santiago," said J. T. "*Profesora,* we need your help with these here boys. We'd like to know where they came from and what happened on Mr. Tillis Geech's shrimp boat."

The *señora was* dressed for school in a modestly dark dress with a white collar. She nodded and turned to the boys and questioned them softly for a few minutes.

Rose Ida kept asking, "What's goin' on? What are they sayin'?"

Finally, the teacher looked up. She said, "This is Ernesto and his brother Tomás Diaz. They are from Cuba. What they are telling me I think is the truth. I too am from Cuba. I was in college in the United States when Castro took power. My husband is in the navy now. He did not want me to come to your house. He is not supposed to be political. After the …

"The Bay of Pigs," offered Grady.

"*Sí*, the Bay of Pigs. They left Cuba on Captain Geech's boat for Miami."

"So Daddy's alive! Grady Geech did you know about this?" Mozelle asked her uncle. "It's true. You knew it all along. *How could you?*"

"Mozelle, I …" Grady bowed his head and tried to escape to the kitchen. He leaned on Kate's deep-dive freezer, shaking his head.

Hands on her hips, Mozelle crowded him. "Did you go down there?" she said.

"Hush." Grady pleaded. "The deputy."

"Oh, shit. Tell me. Tell me now, Uncle Grady, or I swear I'll put your head in this here freezer and close the lid. What have you two been up to?"

"Mozelle, back in the twenties, your grandpa—" Grady began.

"I don't want to hear about Grandpa and the High Sheriff. Or rum-runnin' to Cuba or any other tall tale you want to tell. I want to hear about what you and my daddy have been up to. Right here, right now. I want to know where Daddy is."

Grady answered the last question first. "Tillis lost the boat in a card game."

"I get it. Daddy lost the boat, but it did a Lassie-Come-Home to Little Dog Key. Uncle Grady, I have a better idea. I'm goin' to drive you out to Horse Hole and shoot you." She stalked back into the living room."

The school teacher tried to explain. "*Señora* Mozelle, the boys say Captain Geech and the others left the boat in Jacksonville. The boys stayed aboard because Captain Geech going to take them to their uncle. *¿Donde, Ernesto?*"

"Tybee Island."

Grady decided to come clean. "Castro has been lettin' exiles pick up relatives at Camarioca. Couple of years back, Tillis and I went down there to pick up some money. Shrimpin' had been bad. Seemed like a good way to … well, earn some cash by rentin' out the boat to an exile group. So last year, Tillis came up short. Had a pretty good year myself. But you know your daddy. And it was Christmas.…"

Rose Ida demanded, "How did these boys end up on Little Dog Key?"

Señora Santiago broke in, "When Captain Geech did not come back to the boat, they sailed it north. They say they can do this, following the coast line. They are … How do you say it in English? Grease Monkeys. They fish and run the boats all the time in Cuba. There was a storm. They drifted. Then they ran aground."

Mozelle had to have the last word. "So what you are tellin' me is these boys stole the boat Daddy lost at cards and Daddy is in Miami too embarrassed to come home and face Mama."

"'Bout the size of it," Grady confessed.

AUGUST 18, 1969

Two days later, just where Highway 17 turned south toward Savannah, Rose Ida caught a glimpse of the Tallmadge Memorial Bridge and stopped her car slap in the middle of the road. On the left was a yellow stucco building fronted by an enormous black cat. "Krazy Katz Fireworks," the sign read. On the right, an equally large sign, but it said "Loco Joe's" and was a watermelon shade of pink.

"I can't," Rose Ida said in a voice like a gypsy violin rosined with honeysuckle. "Just can't cross that bridge."

The bridge loomed like a shark fin from the expanse of Spartina grass. Clouds banked ominously around the structure.

"What do you mean, *can't?*" asked Mozelle from the backseat, sitting between the two brothers. She was a woman who had no truck with *can't*. Whining neither. And she was getting hot.

"I just can't drive over that there bridge," Rose Ida said, covering her eyes.

She peeked through fingers, tipped in red polish, over at Kate to see how she was taking it. Kate turned away, giving Rose Ida not an iota of sympathy.

Mozelle filled in the gap. "How are we goin' to get to Savannah? How are we goin' to get our little brown brothers to their *Tío Gordo*?" Mozelle lit a cigarette. It bobbed up and down as she fussed. "I never saw the like. You were the one who was in such an all-fired hurry to take these boys to their kin. Kate was perfectly satisfied to take them in, weren't you, Kate?"

It was true. Kate had bunked them on the twin beds in Sissy's room and clothed them in J. T.'s hand-me-downs. All Rose Ida did was hand over twenty dollars to buy the boys underwear at the PX, declaring they were "far too dusky and fusty" for her.

Mozelle worked the phones, braving the maze of the social service agencies. It was Grady Geech who finally found the Spanish speaking striker on a boat out of Thunderbolt known around the docks as *El Gordo*. The boys had shouted with delight, "*Sí! Sí! Tío Gordo!*"

That brought them to this full stop in the middle of the highway to Savannah. There they sat in Rose Ida's 1968 white Toronado with the red interior. Rose Ida flung the car door open. "You drive, Kate," she said.

Before Kate could reply, Rose Ida was out of the vehicle and stalking across the highway, leaving the car door open.

"Rose Ida," Mozelle called. "Come back."

Rose Ida paused for a moment, rummaged in her purse for a cigarette; then rolled her eyes up at the fireworks sign. She thought better of it. "I'm goin' for a Co'-Cola."

Kate sighed and slid into the driver's seat. She wasn't going over that bridge either. She closed the door and restarted the car. She put on the blinkers for a left turn, looked both ways, and pulled into Krazy Katz Fireworks. She had to admit that everyone seemed happier to have the Tallmadge Memorial Bridge behind them. Mozelle climbed over Ernesto and got out of the car. She leaned against the driver-side door and stretched. Kate rolled her window down. "We should have waited for your uncle Grady to take these boys," she said. "I think we ought to go back. I don't mind. With Sissy at college and J. T. either in class or at football practice, there's nobody at home."

"What about Ted?"

"You know Ted. He doesn't mind."

Ernesto rolled his window down. Mozelle grinned and tapped him on the nose. "Y'all right, *hermano*? We are surely slow about getting you to *Tío Gordo*."

The boy's dark eyes danced. His brother squeezed alongside. "*Sí, Señora* Mozelle. What you say. Okay."

"Don't understand a word I'm sayin', do you? I don't like the look of that sky either, Kate," said Mozelle.

Rose Ida finally returned with a six pack of cold cola and a bag of chips. She found a church key in the glove box, opened the bottles, and handed them out.

"Better?" asked Mozelle. "Scoot over, Ernie," she said as she got in the backseat. She opened the bag of chips and offered them first to the boys. They dug in. "Hold on. Let's share," she said.

Rose Ida slid into the front passenger seat, tucking one leg under her and turning to face Mozelle. "Ready?"

Mozelle passed the chips to her, but Rose Ida refused with a frown. "We can drive through the wildlife sanctuary and Port Wentworth. We'll have these boys home in a jiffy," Rose Ida said. She rummaged in her purse and came up with a wax paper bag. Inside were a moist hanky and two diaper pins. The smell of bleach filled the interior as she wiped her hands. Then she carefully cleaned the outside of the bottle of cola.

It was raining by the time Kate pulled on to the highway. In her rearview mirror, she could see the clouds hiding the top reaches of the bridge. A gust of wind pushed them along. By the time they reached the wildlife sanctuary, the rain was sheeting off the windshield. The tide was in, and water was nearly to the road: the potholes were filled. Although it was only one o'clock in the afternoon, Kate needed her headlights. The inside of the car was humid and smoke-filled, moisture condensing on the glass. They played with the windows to adjust for the rain, heat, and smoke.

Kate blew out a breath, fogging the windshield. She bit her lip and reached forward to wipe the glass. She couldn't see the lane markings. "I know, but it's slow goin'. I wish Ted were here. I hate drivin' in the rain."

Rose Ida fiddled with the radio dial. "Leroy Blue said we were in for weather. Y'all know he's right about storms. You suppose this here Camille changed course?"

"We got tornado watches and gale warnin's," snapped Mozelle. "Why do you think Uncle Grady wouldn't take me down on the boat?"

The radio announcer droned the latest bulletin on Hurricane Camille's track onshore. "Residents of one beachfront condominium decided to stay and enjoy a hurricane when their high-rise building collapsed. All but three were killed.… One survivor plucked from a tree some five miles inland. Now, turning to Debbie, tracking way, way out there. A fish storm, but affecting rip currents all …"

Rose Ida shut him up midsentence. "Anna, Blanch, Camille. Now *Debbie?* Why can't we have a *him*acane, for once? Uh huh?"

Rose Ida turned all the way around this time, kneeling in the front seat but remembering to tug her mini skirt modestly. She breathed smoke into Ernesto's face. "Tell me the truth, now Mozelle. You really goin' to learn to shrimp? You can't do that. Who ever heard of a woman shrimper? You can't. It's not done."

"Of course, I can. Uncle Grady is showin' me the ropes," Mozelle answered. "He's showin' me how to navigate."

"Still, a woman out of the Landings and Little Dog Key?" Rose Ida settled back into the seat, blowing smoke at Kate. "I do foretell there will be *talk.*"

Kate frowned and cranked the side window down a bit.

Rose Ida continued, "Navigation. Isn't that math—trigonometry or somethin'? As I recall, you were never very good at math in school."

"This is different. Uncle Grady let me look at his *snag* book. Besides, when you sail the same waters, you get to know the way the marsh and the water look. High tide. Low tide. You feel it. You taste it. You know your home."

"Like the loggerhead and salmon," said Kate.

"Exactly. When Gunny retires, he can sail with us. Leroy Blue's boy is up and comin'. He'd sign on as striker, handle the nets and doors. 'Course my girls would help."

"Nasty man, Mr. Leroy. In a foul mood since the sheriff found his still. Least that's what I hear," said Rose Ida.

Both Mozelle and Kate ventured to laugh.

"And you can't take that boy on neither," continued Rose Ida.

Mozelle was indignant. "Can't? Can't? Of course I can."

Rose Ida jabbed her lipstick-stained cigarette in the ash tray. She pulled her makeup bag out of her purse. "Kate, don't your boy fish with him?" She applied color to her lips using the rearview mirror. "Seems like J. T. was always talkin' about Mr. Leroy."

Kate gripped the steering wheel hard. "When we first came to Elijah's Landing, J. T. would go out when the mule and wagon came by. Never seen a mule. Never seen a wagon," Kate said.

"Never seen a black man, neither," Rose Ida put in tartly.

Kate adjusted the mirror. She could see the boys. They had big brown eyes like her son's. They were getting restless, trading little jabs and pokes. She continued with her story, "So J. T. asked Mr. Leroy where he lived. Mr. Leroy said 'At Land's End.' And J. T. said, 'At the end of the world?' Mr. Leroy looked at him and considered. 'No. The *center of the universe.*'"

Rose Ida was not impressed. "Now I have got to pee," she said.

"Rose Ida," Mozelle admonished from the backseat before Kate could. "Language."

"How ever do you say it in Spanish? I'm all up to my eyeballs. Oh wait. Stop, Kate. There's Williamsport Seafood. Pull in. We'll get a shrimp basket."

Kate braked in a spray of water, sending Rose Ida lurching forward. Rose Ida piled out, stepping into a puddle. Shaking out her sandals like a wet tabby, she headed for the door of the restaurant.

Mozelle followed her but put up her hand to stop the boys from getting out. "Stay here," she said.

"Mozelle," called Kate. "Surely these boys have got to go and are hungry, too."

Mozelle was adamant, "You know Rose Ida. We'll send somethin' out," she said.

"Well I'm not leaving them out here."

"Kate."

"Oh, ding dong! Let me take them to the little boys' room. Or are they too brown to pee inside?" asked Kate, irritated.

Mozelle compromised. "I'll use the pay phone and call the dock. Maybe someone can come get them. This storm is gettin' worse. It's the least they can do," she said.

Kate shepherded the boys to the men's room, risking her dignity to peek inside. The coast was clear. She scampered to the ladies' room and came out as quickly as she could, shaking her hands to air dry. The boys were jumping puddles. "Don't get your clothes all wet and muddy," she called automatically. "Did you wash your hands?" She stopped herself with a little laugh, wondering how Cuban mothers nagged. "Get in," she said instead, putting Tomás in the front, next to her.

Kate pulled out the coloring book and crayons that Mozelle had gotten him. As Tomás turned the pages, Kate asked him, "What's this?"

In a little while, Mozelle came out with sweet tea, two kid-sized baskets of fried fish, and one with shrimp for Kate. "You're lucky to get lunch. The lights just went out in the restaurant," said Mozelle. Kate started the car to listen to the radio.

Mozelle got in the front and boosted Tomás to the back. A gust of wind rocked the car. Rain clattered like sea spray. "It's like bein' on the boat," said Mozelle.

"You really love shrimping, don't you?" Kate asked.

"Since I was a girl. My sister wouldn't have dared. But I did. I'd haul on my rubber boots and set out after Daddy and Uncle Grady. Daddy'd put out the *try-net* every twenty minutes. I would do the count for them. When they pulled up the nets and started culling and heading the catch, the sea gulls would come. I flung the heads and trash fish to the wind. The gulls would come to me."

"What about your daddy?"

Mozelle shifted in the seat. She said, "Daddy's made his bed, Kate. I don't want to talk about it."

Kate touched her friend's arm. "That's all you have talked about. And his boat," she said softly. She sighed, "At least you know what you want."

Mozelle stole shrimp from Kate's basket. "I have the boat. It's mine. I feel the wind in my face, taste the salt," she said, wiping her fingers on a napkin. She turned off the annoying static from the radio. "I have a small ship and a star to steer her by." She laughed ... and then sobered. "Uncle Grady says you need prudence and patience to shrimp."

Kate laughed. "Prudence and Patience," Kate repeated, changing the emphasis. "I swear you Southerners come up with the strangest names for your kids. I'm glad I'm just plain Kate."

"Oh, I didn't mean it that way. But you're right. I do need my twins, Prudence and Patience, with capital Ps. But I do have what I want. What do you want?"

"I want ... what do I want? A snug house, never having to move again. A long life to do good deeds in," Kate said.

"Just like the old Puritans."

"That's me, good old Yankee Kate. I still say *pahk* the *cah* in the *yahd*, don't I?"

"I still need a translation. Speakin' of translation, what do these boys want?" Mozelle glanced at the boys in back who were polishing off their lunch.

"*¿Qué quieres, hermanos?*" asked Kate.

"America, *Tío Gordo*," the boys chorused.

Mozelle said, "You have enjoyed the brothers back there."

"I guess so. But Rose Ida ... she doesn't want them near her. She's always talking about how they smell. They cleaned up well enough. They're smart. Imagine sailing the boat all the way up here. Maybe it's because she doesn't have children," said Kate.

"Don't you know about her kid?" Mozelle asked.

"What kid?"

Mozelle seemed delighted to gossip. "Her daughter from her first marriage to *the General*. She *mislaid* her."

Kate was incredulous. "What do you mean, mislaid her? She lost her? We've known Rose Ida for over ten years. This is the first I've heard about a child. Did the baby die?"

"Well, no, not exactly lost her. From what I hear, the divorce was messy and her ex got custody. Strange, a mother not gettin' the baby."

Kate agreed. "There are a couple of things strange about Rose Ida."

"Well, losin' a kid could mess anybody up. She should be about nineteen or twenty now."

They considered the future in silence. It was quiet in the backseat. Kate adjusted the rearview mirror to see the boys. The seat was a jumble of crayons, napkins, and french fries with ketchup drying on Rose Ida's red upholstery.

Finally Mozelle said, "I better get back inside." She got out of the car but leaned back in, grinning. "Rose Ida will be wipin' down the tables and inspectin' the kitchen."

Kate said, "I wonder what Rose Ida wants."

Mozelle said, "She wants somethin' to spike her sweet tea!"

A blue Ford pickup pulled in and parked. The driver, a red-headed man, got out, rounded the back of the truck, and stomped up to Mozelle. He smiled as best he could with a wad of tobacco in his cheek. His blue eyes were kind. The stranger rocked back on his heels a bit. He asked, "You Mozelle Seabrook?"

Mozelle hesitated. The sun broke through the clouds. They were on the good side of the hurricane goddess after all. She raised her hand to shade her eyes as she studied him. "Yes," Mozelle told him, "Did you come about Ernesto and Tomás?"

Another man got out of the truck. He was heavy set and dark, all smiles and teeth. He answered, "*Sí. Muchachos, vámonos.*"

The boys lit up and started getting out of the car. Mozelle asked the boy's uncle, color rising in her face, "Do you know where my father is? I know he's around here somewhere." She stomped her foot. "He probably set the boat adrift himself." She pushed past the two men heading to their truck. "Daddy? You in the truck, hidin' from me?"

Kate pulled the key out of the ignition and got out of the car. "Mozelle, stop …" She reached for her friend's arm.

Mozelle shook her off and slammed her open hand against the side of the truck. She flung the door open. "Daddy?"

There was no one inside. The blue-eyed man stood aside. Red-faced, he held out an envelope to Mozelle. "This is for you, Mrs. Seabrook.

Mozelle pushed his hand away, and the envelope fell to the ground. "No. You just tell Daddy thanks for sendin' two little boys to do a man's job." She stalked to the restaurant door.

Ernesto picked up the envelope and handed it to Kate. Her Yankee nature could never refuse money. She hugged him. Kate said to the two men, "They are beautiful boys. They were no trouble. Their things are in the trunk. They had nothing but the clothes they were wearing. We got them some clean clothes. Underwear, shorts, shirts. Coloring books." Kate realized she was babbling. Her hand shook as she inserted the key into the trunk lock. "Come inside. You should talk to Mozelle. She's just worried about her father."

"No. I can't. Give her this. It might explain.... Then maybe not. The important thing is these boys are with kin and are safe."

"What about Mozelle's kin? What about her father?"

The man shrugged. He moved quickly for his size, shepherding the boys and their uncle along. Ernesto and Tomás climbed into the bed of the truck with their gear. They waved, and they were gone.

Kate sighed. She could see Mozelle in the window of Williamsport Seafood. She turned the key to start the engine. It wouldn't turn over.

Rose Ida was hanging on to the pay phone as Kate entered the restaurant. She twisted the phone cord. "Aubrey, I told you not to …" She pouted, pulling at her hair, eyes like blackberry jam, mascara running. "But, Aubrey …" she sighed, stroking the receiver.

Mozelle sat in a booth jabbing her straw into her tea. As Kate slid in beside her, the tea glass tipped. Mozelle made a grab for it. "Damn, damn," she said between clenched teeth.

Kate mopped up. "The car won't start. I'll call Ted when Rose Ida gets off the phone. Why didn't you say good-bye to the boys?" she said all at once.

They could hear Rose Ida's laugh, rising up to a hysterical pitch.

"She's upset." Mozelle's words were clipped. Her face was pale. She bit her lip.

The waitress came up, ticking her pencil against her pad. "Can I get you somethin'? We got plenty of tea and coleslaw. And whatever was up from before them lights went out. Better eat it up before we have to toss the lot."

"Just tea, please," Kate said to the waitress. Nodding toward the lobby where Rose Ida's laughter rang out. "Rose Ida sounds *really* upset," she said.

Mozelle said, "She's upset about them leavin'. Me, too. They were the last to see my daddy, I guess. But, Kate, she told me somethin'. You'll never guess. About her daughter."

Kate interrupted her. "I took this for you," she said, handing the envelope to Mozelle. "Did you recognize him? Stupid me, I didn't even ask his name. Do you think we broke any laws—just handing them off like that?" Kate paused, "Mozelle? Mozelle, what is it?"

Mozelle slid a knife under the flap of the envelope. A stack of twenties slid out wrapped in a strip of paper. She unfolded the note. It wasn't signed, but she recognized her father's handwriting. She read it aloud to Kate. "Help your mother. I got a salvage job out of Miami. Take care of my boat."

Mozelle contemplated the fan of money on the table. "I guess that is that," she sighed. "Forget about callin' Ted. I suppose we can get someone to help us here. We're not helpless, you know."

Rose Ida announced, "We need to get on back to Elijah's Landing, uh-huh. That there boat of yours has sunk, and I don't know what all will happen next."

AUGUST 19, 1969

Kate missed out on the drama unfolding at Rose Ida's. The shades were drawn. She did heard folks whispering at church. Rose Ida's name was passed along with the communion ware and the offering plate. But Kate missed the content and, good Yankee that she was, decided to let it go. She and Ted did go down to the dock to see the wreck of Mozelle's shrimp boat, the *Sweet Mozelle,* sunk to the gunwales, hanging by her tie lines like a drowning sailor clutching a life preserver. Not till the next morning, promptly at 9:00 a.m., did Rose Ida call and give any sort of a hint that trouble was afoot. Kate thought she sounded a little shrill and agitated for that early in the morning.

Rose Ida started right in. "Best not tell Mozelle she can't do a thing, for she will do just that," Rose Ida said. "Telling her she *must not*,will just be a challenge to that gal," she fumed.

"What happened?" Kate asked politely.

"Sure enough, some fool asked her what she goin' to do with her daddy's stove-in shrimp trawler. Mozelle told them she goin' to raise the boat, trim out the hole as a door, plug in the freezer and sell shrimp out of the thing."

"That sounds like a good plan," was all Kate could think of to say.

"Uh-huh," Rose Ida huffed. "'You can't do that, Mozelle honey.' I told her. Uh-huh," she declared, as if that would end the matter. "I do foretell there will be talk."

Mozelle called with the rest of the gossip. "Did you hear Rose Ida's daughter turned up on her doorstep? With a *newborn*?"

Kate was speechless as Mozelle rattled away. "Mrs. Polk told me at church. She heard the whole argument while she was watering her tomatoes. It seems that her daughter arrived *last week* with the child! Rose Ida wouldn't let her in, told her to report to *the General*. While we were in Savannah, Aubrey took them in, but the daughter refused to stay. She just left the baby with Aubrey and *skedaddled*. She didn't want her father—the General—to know!"

When Mozelle finally rang off, Kate dialed Rose Ida's number. The phone rang ten, eleven times. Kate went down the hall and climbed in the bathtub and stood tip-toe so she could peer out her window at Rose Ida's front door.

Kate sighed. She rummaged through her linen closet until she found the box labeled "Sɪssʏ's Baʙʏ Cʟoᴛʜᴇs." Behind the box, she found a square long-necked bottle that Ted had hidden. She tucked the bottle under her arm, hefted the box, and resolutely crossed the road.

"Rose Ida, Rose Ida!" she called. "Open up. I know you're in there. Open this door!"

When Rose Ida opened the door, she wasn't dressed to her usual nines, although her white capris and halter top were pristine and her gypsy earrings jangled. It was the *burp cloth* that did the outfit in. Like a corsage, the infant in her arms squalled pink, quickening with outrage. Rose Ida looked at Kate and said, "Well, aren't y'all Christmas in July."

Kate reached for the child, and Rose Ida for the gin.

"It's August," Kate said. "It's hurricane season."

SHRIMP AND PAN-FRIED GRITS

Dayclear Morning
take grits left over
and pat them flat
Smooth them out some
cool them down

Noon
Catch some shrimp in your net

Suppertime
Slice them grits into squares
and slide into hot grease
Ease them out the skillet
when they be brown on the edges
Throw onion into the grease
then the shrimp
Just a minute and a bit
Spoon the shrimp and onion
over them fried grits.

Photo by Marge Boyle

THE POSSUM LAUGHED

AUGUST 28, 1979
DAVID

Leroy Blue and his granddaughter rocked on the porch of the old hall and parlor house he'd rented on Mr. Wallace's property. Janey Blue was a bright-skinned child of six, a puzzle of three races. She copied the old man's every move as he dozed in the noontide heat. "Pap Roy, is there goin' to be a storm today?" inquired Janey.

"What's that?" Mr. Leroy asked. He was going blind, losing his teeth, but his hearing was fine. Mr. Leroy had given up his mule and vegetable wagon when sugar prices dropped. Beer in aluminum cans had cut into his profits. He just wanted to rest now. "Hush now, Possum. It too hot to talk."

Janey was indignant. "I ain't no possum."

"You is too. Your mamma be the greatest grandchild of the Alligator Lady."

"Ain't no Alligator Lady," the little girl pouted.

Mr. Leroy chuckled, not going for the argument. Moving onto the porch room was not a hardship since his daughter-in-law, Raephine, was hardly ever at home. By day, Raephine worked in the homes of ladies on the Point. By night, she was a cook at a juke joint called the Bloody Bucket. He had Janey all to himself. The hardship was the loss of Junior, his son. Damned if the boy wasn't nearly the next to the last Marine killed pulling

57

out of Saigon. Janey was his treasure. He gave in. "Are too," he said. He sat up when a car door slammed.

Kate Forester picked her way through the wire gate. The hound dog panted, too hot to do anything other than open a red eye and twitch a nostril at the white lady with Mamie Eisenhower bangs and sensible shoes. Stepping in her tracks, carrying the tin foil–wrapped plate, was ten-year-old Camille Tisdale. Kate tried to make her hello sound like Low-Country greeting but Massachusetts crept into her vowels and mismanaged her *r*'s. "Hello, Mr. Leroy. I have your lunch."

Mr. Leroy roused, "Who's comin'? Who is the child?"

Camille spoke up, "I'm Camille Tisdale. Rose Ida Tisdale is my auntie."

The child handed the plate to Mr. Leroy. To Kate he said, "Thank you, Mrs. *Come-Here*. Most grateful." He used the designation used by Gullah folk for newcomers. He and Janey had always *been-here*, Kate had *come-here*. Although, she had lived on Catbrier Lane for over twenty years, to those born in the Low Country, she was still an outsider.

To the child he said, "Well hey, I know your grandma. She likes her shrimp and cane juice. You be the child called after the hurricane. Hurricane Camille meet little Possum Child."

Both little girls started to say at the same time, "My name ain't—" but collapsed into giggles. Janey ran down the steps. She motioned for Camille to follow. The two disappeared around the side of the house.

Kate, giving her best imitation of a sweet southern smile, said to Mr. Leroy, "We brought you some extra corn bread like you asked. I think the hospital made greens with a piece of meat but ding-dong if I know what kind. There is some pie and sweet tea."

Mr. Leroy grumbled, "Ain't no more makin' cane juice for me. Dixie Crystal be cheaper. The beer be too. Them aluminum cans keep it cold, but it be like drinkin' Kool-Aid," Mr. Leroy said.

"How is Raephine?" asked Kate.

"Raephine is one I never figured out." Mr. Leroy moved uneasily in the rocking chair. He said, "When it time for cryin' and weepin', she done be laughin' and dancin'. She left the child with an old man like me. Who will look after her when I die?"

Kate hesitated.

The old man wiped the sweat from his face with a bandana. He continued half to himself, "My doin'. All that cane juice. All my fault. Still she's the Alligator Lady's gal. Raephine will come aroun' even if she kind of just backs into doin' the right thing. What do you think, Mrs. *Come-Here*? Will you watch over little Possum Child while Raephine weeps?"

Kate told him, "Don't worry. Isn't that what you told me about hurricanes? Things will work themselves out."

As Kate drove off, Mr. Wallace came down Pigtown Alley in his big black Cadillac. He blocked Kate, splaying the car across the road. He maneuvered his huge bulk across the dirt road, greeting Kate. "Hot," he said, wiping his brow.

Kate believed it was.

"You've been down to Mr. Leroy's? Now look here, Mrs. Forester, I thought I told you church ladies this here alley is private property. You got no need to be on my property. Old Mr. Leroy's time is comin'. Sooner the better if you ask me. He's got a place here until he dies, but that there gal, Raephine. I can't have it. I am not havin' that kind of goin's-on out here."

"What kind of goings on?" Kate asked.

He ignored her. He said, "Now I know, you're not from around here. Maybe you don't know how things are. Mr. Leroy is a good man, in his place." He had to take a breath. Then he asked, "That Rose Ida Tisdale's girl? What would Mrs. Tisdale think of you bringin' her down here?"

"I expect she would think I was doing the Lord's work."

Mr. Wallace said, "I'm warnin' you. All you do-gooders better stay out of my alley.

Camille asked in a very loud child's voice, "What does it mean—'in his place'?"

Mr. Wallace grew red. He swelled up to speak again. He changed his mind and tramped back to his car. He pulled around Kate, who nodded in her do-gooder, outside agitator, and blankety-blank-lover's way. She didn't smile.

Camille said, "Tell me a story about the Alligator Lady."

The tales of the Alligator Lady were older than dirt and Kate had heard them from the time she arrived in the Low Country. She had been a tall woman of color, dark red clay, with the high cheekbones of a Cherokee, long limbs out of Africa. She knew the lore of the Indian and the root of the black. Her hair was straight and shiny. She kept it wrapped under a scarf. She talked to the gators living in the rice paddy on Mr. Wallace's pig farm. A possum was her *familiar*.

Kate, a Yankee who didn't believe in such things as root, hex, and spell, couldn't resist the hurricane story. So when Camille wished for a story, Kate said, "The year of the Great Hurricane, 1893, the Alligator Lady was a young wife with a babe and a fat husband by the name of Greene. The cabin was snug, with a sleeping loft.

"The Alligator Lady could see things where others couldn't. She could hear stuff nobody listened for. She said to her man the evening before the Great Hurricane, 'We got to leave this island.'

"'Oh, hush up, woman,' Green told her and went possum hunting.

"She took Greene's ax, which before the birth of the baby, had been under the bed. She cut a little fire wood and talked to Ole Possum by the wood pile. Ole Possum was a firm believer in keeping friends close and enemies … like Greene … closer. Possum told the Alligator Lady to put the ax and a rope in the rafters. She gave Possum a bit of corn bread and bacon grease, pointed out the direction Greene had gone. She bid him good evening.

"The next morning, outside of the Praise House, the Alligator Lady had a seizure. She fell on the ground singing out, 'Got to leave this place.' The sisters gathered around mistook her words for a shout.

"The storm came, and the waters rose. The Alligator Lady used the ax to chop a hole in the roof. Greene, nearly too fat to get through, clung to the ridgeline and the chimney. The Alligator Lady rolled the child into her skirt and bound the little one to her chest with her head wrap. Her braids fell to her waist, and she wound them around her body for good measure and climbed on to the roof. Possum clung to a tree and urged her onward. When the storm subsided and the waters receded, the Alligator Lady, Possum, and child praised God and his tree. There be no sign of Greene. The possum laughed."

Camille asked, "Was it a boy hurricane or a girl hurricane?"

Mozelle's Porch

The sight of the little shrimp boat on Mozelle Seabrook's front lawn made Kate smile. Rose Ida said the place looked like a tawdry boarding house with the ark parked out front. The house itself was sited with its shy, narrow shoulder facing Old Shell Road in prim Low Country fashion. It had a false door and blue shutters concealing the veranda. The door was for gentlemen callers. Most everybody trooped up the marsh-side stairs. The long, cool porch caught the breezes when the tide changed. It was vined with wisteria, shrimp nets, and ladies' unmentionables. It did seem like a boarding house with Geech aunts and daughters looking for husbands, daughters looking for a respite from husbands, daughters looking to get a divorce, and of course, Mozelle.

Rose Ida liked to invite herself. She reclined on the wicker chairs in an attractive arrangement. She put her wrist on her forehead and whispered most desperately, "Oh law. Oh law. Oh, oh law," until somebody came up with a cool drink or some hot gossip.

Rose Ida played the vamp, but Mozelle Seabrook lived life like a poem. She moved in with her mother after her husband died, but she determined not to live like a wedding photo torn in half. After the birth of her third daughter, Petula, six months younger than Rose Ida's Camille, she set out to remake her life.

She renamed her father's boat, *Mozelle's Girls*, despite Rose Ida's stern warnings that bad luck would follow. There it stood on Old Shell Road, the beached shrimp boat, a covered picnic pavilion; a few crab tables, and a grill: Mozelle's Market, a hard-won enterprise.

Kate parked the car and Camille lit out, yelling for Petula.

"Act like a lady," Kate admonished, to no avail.

From the veranda, Rose Ida called to Kate, "Did you see Mozelle's new sign? 'Mozelle's Shrimp Bait Beer.' No commas. Who on God's green earth would drink Bait Beer?" Rose Ida asked. She waved an ice tea spoon at Kate. Whatever she was drinking in the Bama Jelly glass wasn't iced tea. "I can't believe she put the commercial beer cooler in Mrs. Geech's front room."

Kate sat on the step and fanned herself. Her face felt taunt. She trembled. She watched the wind cross the Spartina marsh. A great blue heron speared a fish. Finally, she said, "Mr. Wallace and I had a discussion about Mr. Leroy."

"Didn't I tell you to stay out of Pigtown?" Rose Ida said. She raised her voice to a hog-calling level. "Camille, Petula. Girls, get on out here."

In a moment there was a clatter down hidden stairs. The screen door banged. "Yes?" Camille and Petula shouted together, and then they giggled.

"Mrs. Kate needs a song to raise her spirits. Sing the one I taught you," Rose Ida ordered.

The girls kicked off their shoes and did cartwheels in the grass. As Rose Ida conducted with the ice tea spoon they began to sing. The tune was a fractured version of "The Old Hundred" with a little hand jazz and a childish bump and grind.

> Praise God for this blessed view.
> Praise God for all the creatures too.
> Praise Him for the rising tide,
> For shrimp that below abide—

Petula broke off, shading her eyes. "Shrimp boats. Here comes Momma."

The girls switched tempo and gave Kate a chorus of "Shrimp boats are a'comin'." They broke into a run, heading for the dock.

"Home is the sister, home from the sea," Rose Ida murmured.

Kate felt a sisterly peace come over her. In a moment though, she began to hunger for her little house on Catbrier Lane and her own sweet Ted.

SEPTEMBER 3, 1979

MR. LEROY'S PORCH

Kate knew. She put Camille behind her. "Stay here," Kate told her.

The girl bucked at the gesture, but she was a biddable child. She did as she was told. She raised her chin, taking in the scent like a long-legged filly. She shied back two more steps.

Somewhere below the smell of the pigs, the burned and rotting garbage, Kate detected the grim odor. The old dog must have died under the porch, she decided. She approached cautiously. "Mr. Leroy, we have your lunch."

Janey sat forlorn on the steps, her knees drawn up. Her eyes filled with tears.

A blue-bottle fly buzzed Kate. "What's the matter, Janey? Where is Mr. Leroy?" Kate asked, but she knew. "Corruption of the flesh," she almost intoned aloud like some old-timey prophet.

"He asleep. He can't be 'sturbed," Janey told her.

Kate offered her hand to the girl. "Where is your mother? Is she here?"

Janey said, "On the floor. She won't get up, neither."

Kate caught her breath and let it out carefully. "Janey, go sit in the car," she said softly. "You know Camille. Go sit with her."

Kate peered through the screen door of the sleeping porch. She could see his profile, dark and still, the flies settling. What had made him Leroy Blue was gone. His face was no more animated than the produce on her shopping list: eggplant, grapes, plums. He had been the vegetable man. Twenty years back, he told her, "Mrs. *Come-Here*, never sugar the grits. Put hot sauce in the greens. Cook okra with tomatoes—it cuts the slime."

Kate explained rutabaga. Never once did she buy his cane juice. She prayed, "Watch, oh God, with those who ... weep, and give angels charge of those who sleep."

The woman across the way stood on her porch. She was a big woman who looked like an upholstered stack of tires, one each for bosom, belly, and behind. When she crossed the alley as Kate called her, the tires rolled and dipped as she moved. "What's the trouble? Oh, sweet Jesus, it's Mr. Leroy, ain't it? Mr. Wallace, he'll have a fit if Mr. Leroy done died in his house. Where's Raephine? Best get her on out before Mr. Wallace gets here."

Kate asked, "Do you have a phone? I don't want to go inside or touch anything."

"Lord Jesus," the neighbor moaned as she peered in at Mr. Leroy. "Lord have mercy on a poor sinner. Lord have mercy. Mr. Leroy claimed if the Lord turned water into wine, why couldn't he turn corn into—" she made a chugalug sound.

She turned to the kitchen screen. "Where's Raephine?" She opened the kitchen door then slammed it quickly. "Raephine done kill herself. Oh, oh, blood all over the kitchen floor," she wailed. "You best call for an ambulance. They ain't comin' down this alley for the like of me. You call Mr. Wallace. Oh Lordy, you call Mr. Wallace. I'll look after the girls."

Kate made the call. Then she called Rose Ida Tisdale. She did not call Mr. Wallace.

The fire truck made the run up Pigtown Alley, followed by the modified pickup, serving the paramedics. Dr. Julian Otis, the coroner, arrived next.

Dr. Otis was one cool drink of water. Kate watched as he got out of his car, extending each elegant trouser leg and straightening to his full height. He wore an ice-cream suit—the full white-linen regalia except he had loosened the tie and opened his collar. He wiped his brow with a snowy handkerchief. His eyes were the color of ice cubes. "Ma'am," he addressed Kate Forester in a courtly tone.

"I believe Mr. Leroy has died," Kate said hesitantly. "Perhaps his daughter-in-law, too."

"He picked a warm day to do it. I do hope this heat is just our earthly weather and not conditions at his destination," Dr. Otis said.

Kate frowned. "Judge not that ye shall not be judged," she said just as solemnly.

He leaned toward her. Then she could see the sweat stains under the arms of the jacket. It was wrinkled and yellowed. Sweat showed in streaks along the front of his slacks. There were other spots, a most alarming shade of red. He smelled antiseptic, but also of things lurking on the undersides of bandages. "I do not judge," he said. "I am the coroner. I mostly clean up the messes. Pardon me."

Kate stood aside.

Dr. Otis did his diagnosing on the same side of the screen as Kate did. "All right boys," he said. "Load this one up. Natural causes." He begged Kate's pardon again and crossed the porch to the kitchen screen door. "Ah, this gal I know. Raephine?" He called her name loudly, prodding her with his toe.

It was the final straw for Kate. "Dr. Otis," she said in her most disapproving tone.

A paramedic knelt beside the young woman, who sprawled on her stomach. She wore a pale blue maid's uniform. Her hair had escaped its net like an explosion of rusty Brillo pads. A cast-iron skillet was on the floor beside her, the remains of breakfast congealing in what Kate was certain wasn't catsup.

Dr. Otis smiled. If he had been wearing a hat, he would have tipped it to her and bowed. "Epilepsy. She'll be all right. She probably hit her head when she fell out. I can't get these folks to understand they have to take the medicine even when they don't have seizures to prevent havin' them." Dr. Otis turned away.

"I see," Kate said.

Raephine stirred. She sat up. Unseen by Kate, she reached up quick as a black racer snake and swept a small red memo book from the kitchen table. She hid it under her blouse.

One of the paramedics called, "Here comes Mr. Wallace. I believe Mrs. Tisdale is right behind him." They scrambled to get their equipment, anxious to be out of the house before its owner arrived.

Dr. Otis said to Kate, "I have a little paperwork to do for the late Mr. Leroy Blue. Tell the gal to stop by my clinic for a prescription." He looked toward the door where one angry ranting voice could be heard. "Ah, the esteemed Mr. Wallace," Dr. Otis continued, "a man of few words. How creatively he uses the same four letters as noun, verb, and adjective. It is a skill I have not mastered. Good day, Mrs. Forester. Good day, Mr. Wallace."

Henry Wallace ignored the doctor. To Kate he said, "I want this slut out of here. Out. Out. Now.

Right behind him, Rose Ida trooped in. According to Rose Ida, a girl never knew when high heels or a low-cut top would come in handy. The South rolled out of her mouth as smooth as honey or good scotch. "Mr. Wallace, whatever is the problem here?"

The hot air went out of his invectives as if pin-pricked. "Mrs. Tisdale."

Rose Ida sniffed, a small sound like a cat sneezing. "Raephine, what's goin' on?"

Raephine rose, never taking her eyes off Mr. Wallace. Her lips were cracked and bleeding. Her dark amber skin was disfigured by a spreading bruise on her cheek. Blood flowed from her nose, but she seemed unaware of it.

All at once, Kate noticed the frying pan. Kate felt her own body tense as Raephine stood holding it with both hands. "Mr. Leroy passed," Raephine whispered.

Mr. Wallace raised a full hue and cry. "You know what that means: you and your brat are out of here!"

Raephine centered herself. She raised the skillet to head-bashing height. Her eyes narrowed to glittering slits. A large drop of blood spattered to the floor. She was silent.

Wallace started at the gesture, his pig eyes growing wide. "No trouble, you hear?" he said. "But you have to vacate these premises." He held his ground although his jowls quivered.

Kate counted the seconds, holding her breath.

Deftly, Rose Ida stepped into the line of fire, fanning herself with her hands. "I need air," she declaimed. "I do believe I shall faint. Oh, the smell, Mr. Wallace. The smell."

Rose Ida leaned in with all the assets she possessed. She took Wallace's arm and patted it. Wallace took her ample advice. He allowed it was cooler on the porch.

"Raephine," Kate said, "put the skillet down."

The young woman wiped the blood from her chin with a shrug of her shoulder but didn't loosen her grip on the heavy pan. "I ain't no drunk. Slut neither." She looked out the door at Wallace as he took up his case with the fire department. Her lips moved soundlessly. Her eyes rolled back, the muscles in her neck contracted. Her head tilted at an odd angle.

"Raephine," Kate cautioned again. "Let me take you out of here. You are upset now."

Raephine moved slowly to place the skillet on the stove. The old range had a spice shelf above it, a collection of small jars and tins, as well as bunches of herbs hanging from a nail. Raephine shook a gray powder from one tin and chose leaves from the dried herbs.

Kate smelled the strong scent of mint, oregano, and rosemary as Raephine crushed the leaves in her hand. Raephine spit into her palm and clenched her fist. "It's time to go," she whispered. "Where is my Janey?"

"Outside with Mrs. Tisdale and your neighbor," Kate answered.

Raephine staggered and caught herself. Ladles and knives clattered to the floor. Kate steadied the young woman and walked her out of the kitchen.

As they started down the steps, Raephine grabbed the porch railing. She smeared the porch column with the wet herbs and let the remainder fall to the steps. Raephine ground the material into the wood with one foot.

Her neighbor from across the alley carried Janey over. Raephine took her daughter, hugging her tightly.

"Don't you roll your eyes at a white man," the neighbor woman warned. "Don't you mouth him."

Raephine said nothing as she crossed the yard to Kate Forester's car.

As Kate drove away, she looked in her rear view mirror at Raephine and Janey in the backseat. "I hope it wasn't a knife you put under your blouse, Raephine," Kate said.

"No, Mrs. Forester," She pulled out the memo book and passed it forward to Kate. "It's Mr. Wallace's rent book."

Janey called, tugging her mother's arm, "The firemens be burnin' our house."

Kate braked. She leaned out the window looking back at the frame house where Leroy Blue had died. Flames rose as black smoke billowed up into the hot afternoon. She shivered in spite of the heat rising, bending the visible light like a circus mirror.

"Where we goin' to live now?" asked Janey. "What we goin' to do?"

Raephine answered, "I don't know, Possum. I just don't know."

Grimly, Kate put the car in gear. If Rose Ida didn't know, then Mozelle would. She nosed her car down Pigtown Alley on to Old Shell Road to the big house on the marsh.

August 7, 1979
Mozelle's Porch

Kate got up early and took Ted to work. After hearing the weather report about Hurricane David, she decided she had better run to the commissary before the funeral. *A "himacane," just for Camille,* she thought.

Instead, Kate found herself at Mozelle's Market. She looked out to where the marsh, sky, and sea were supposed to be. The unsettling chop to the sea was matched in the sky. The tide was especially high. The red sun broke through the clouds, dazzling her. She covered her eyes with her hand. When the sun spots cleared, she could see the figures under the picnic pavilion. She started toward them. Still partly blinded, she tried to puzzle out what she saw: Rose Ida stretched prone on the top of the picnic table, legs kicked up in pin-up girl fashion.

Rose Ida rolled over and hitched herself to a more ladylike position. She was going to *funeralize* with a nod to Ava Gardner. She wore a black shirtwaist cinched with a broad patent-leather belt. Its flared fullness would cover any deficit in length. Her broad-brimmed hat and heels were on the ground.

Janey squatted on the ground in front of Raephine, examining the bottom of her mother's bare foot. Raephine wore a sleeveless wrapper Kate recognized as belonging to one of Mozelle's twins. Her skin was brass-anklet golden, the sun catching the high cheek bones, the bruise on her face merely shadow. The swelling on her lips had gone down, but there were additional bruises on her bare arms Kate hadn't seen before.

Janey pulled her mother's big toe. Raephine chuckled. Janey moved on to Mozelle's swinging legs. Mozelle's tanned leg beside Raephine's was almost as dark, and the bottoms of both women's feet were pink.

Mozelle wore her shrimping jeans and T-shirt and smelled like it. She'd been out early with Uncle Grady trying to decide which way the hurricane was going to jump. Mozelle said, "Morning Kate. We're playing doctor … or detective. I don't know which."

Janey turned their palms up and studied them. "Open your mouths and stick out your tongues," Janey ordered them gravely.

"Yes, Dr. Possum."

"Mrs. Kate, guess what? They both be the same, Mama and Mrs. Mozelle. On the inside, they just pink. The pinkness be pourin' out they toes and fingers."

"Be careful, Kate," said Rose Ida. "Dr. Possum will operate on you next. Hey, Dr. Possum. Do you think those shoes will fit?"

Janey tried on Rose Ida's black shoes. "Nope," she said gravely.

"Well, hand them here," Rose Ida told her. "Let's go see if Mrs. Geech has some coffee ready. And you, little miss, need to get cleaned up." Rose Ida shook out her skirt and put on her shoes. Then she carefully fitted her hat and snapped the brim. The ladies of the choir would greatly admire Rose Ida's hat as they sang Mr. Leroy home.

Kate said, "Someone has cast a spell on Rose Ida."

Mozelle cut a glance at Raephine.

"Don't look at me," Raephine said softly. "I don't mess with root. Mint and rosemary scents calm the fits."

"Scared Henry Wallace enough to burn your house down, I hear," said Mozelle, making two syllables out of the last word.

Raephine shook her hair. She began to cry. She said, "I ain't got no house. Mr. Wallace burned my clothes. All I got is the clothes I fell down in. This." She gestured to the house dress she wore. "Thanks to you, I got somethin' for Mr. Leroy's funeral."

"We are here for you," Mozelle said. "You are not alone."

"I ain't got no family."

Mozelle said, "My mother's house has many rooms. She took me and my girls in until I could fight my way out of a foxhole after my husband died. With Mr. Leroy gone, maybe you feel that way now," Mozelle said. "Let us be your family. You are a Marine widow. We can help you get some benefits, find you a place."

Raephine said, "Junior and me aren't married true. We just stood up before Reverend Willis. We never got the license."

The three of them sat in silence; church ladies on a pew. The sun ascended for the morning reading. "Red sky at mornin', shrimpers take warnin'," Mozelle said.

Kate took the rent book from her purse. She handed it across Raephine to Mozelle. Mozelle sat quietly with the little memo book in her lap. She opened it and turned a few pages. Then she swung around and put the memo book on the table top to examine it closely. She sighed.

Raephine shivered. She hid her face in her hands with a moan. Suddenly, her limbs were like water. She began to pitch off the bench.

Mozelle blocked her fall. "Hold her head, Kate."

Kate cradled Raephine's head. Her hair was lamb-soft despite its steel-wool appearance, no hairspray but a hint of sassafras. She was fragile as a wren, wings beating. "It's okay, Raephine, we've got you," Kate said.

Rose Ida called from the house, "Coffee's up." She descended the steps, barefoot with red-painted toes. She carried the percolator in one hand and a quart of milk in the other. Behind her streamed a little caravan of raggle-taggle gypsies-o. Camille had a tray of ham biscuits and the sugar bowl. Petula carried two mugs, and Janey brought up the rear with two more.

The distinctive sound of childish giggles and the smell of coffee revived Raephine. Like a mime passing a hand over her face, Raephine's expression changed into a tight mask, her eyes hooded. She took a hairnet out of the pocket of her wrapper and tamped down the Angela Davis excess of hair. The girls set the table. Raephine took the pot of coffee from Rose Ida and began to pour. She offered the ladies biscuits.

Rose Ida declined a biscuit. She sugared up her coffee. "What are we doin' about Raephine?" she asked. The young woman was invisible in a new persona as servant.

Raephine frowned, her expression a protest.

Rose Ida said, "Southerners take care of their folks. A fact Mr. Wallace seems to have forgotten. He is a pig farmer and a pig. First, Raephine has got to quit her job at the Bloody Bucket."

Raephine dug in. "No," she said, hoisting the coffeepot in defiance.

Rose Ida gave a little wave of dismissal. "There's where the trouble began. Folks talk. The Bloody Bucket is not where a respectable gal should be workin'." Rose Ida stopped to light up a cigarette. She soldiered on, still referring to Raephine in the third person. "Some folks don't know the difference between fallin' out and layin' down. Tittle-tattle. Mr. Trouble raises his head. He sniffs out the worst. Oh, that there gal. Somebody's got to be cookin' in the kitchen with Raephine. Ah-hah. A man can get a little brown bread down at the Bloody Bucket. Of course, Mr. Wallace holds the lease."

Mozelle said, "Well, we have got Mr. Wallace's rent book."

Rose Ida said, "Give it here. Let me see." She paused as she read down a page. "Oh law, this isn't Mr. Wallace's red rent book. It's his little *black* book."

"You don't mean," Mozelle said, stifling a laugh.

Raephine drew herself up to her full height. She said, "Some is happy to pay, some is not."

Kate said primly, "I have no ding-dong idea what you are talking about. Give the rent book back to me. I'll take care of this in a ladylike way."

Mozelle stood and swept biscuit crumbs from her jeans. "Let's get our old moonshiner buried first. My mother needs help in the house. I need help in the market. You *can* cook?" Mozelle asked.

Raephine answered, "Give me a seasoned skillet. Show me the grits and shrimp."

"Enough said," Rose Ida agreed.

AUGUST 8, 1979
DR. OTIS'S PORCH

Dr. Otis, the coroner, had a clinic in a shotgun house on Edenboro Avenue. The interior walls had been blown out. The place was clear of all furniture except the line of chairs along each wall and the big desk up front. There was a sink and a rolling chair for Dr. Otis. Dispensary cabinets lined the back wall. The two examination areas were screened off, but gave little privacy. It was like sick call at the drive-in theater. There were no secrets in Dr. Otis's Clinic.

A receptionist ignored patients according to need. The ill and inflamed alike took a seat, mostly young black mothers on the left, the white and elderly on the right.

Kate sighed. Mozelle sighed.

Rose Ida bustled right along, pulling Raephine up to the desk. "All this gal needs is a prescription. It will just take a minute. Oh, Dr. Otis," Rose Ida waved as Dr. Otis looked up from his patient. "I brought Raephine in just like you told us."

When the receptionist stood up, she was formidable. Rose Ida ignored her, guiding Raephine to the right. She selected a chair next to a blue-haired lady and told Raephine to sit. A stir passed through the patients, but even the receptionist hesitated to declare that Raephine sat on the wrong side of the clinic. Rose Ida said, "Raephine, this is Mrs. Polk. She lost her husband in 1944. He was a Marine, too. Mrs. Polk, Raephine's husband was killed in the Vietnam."

Mrs. Polk was short-sighted, with cataracts milky in her blue eyes. She turned to Raephine and took her hand. "My dear," she said softly. "Take heart. Time will heal."

Kate sat down next to Raephine. She whispered, "I guess you think we are three old biddies. We're poking our noses in where we aren't wanted. Raephine, I know it seems unfair J. T. got home and Leroy Junior didn't. You think, *Right, the white boy lived and the colored boy didn't.*"

Behind Rose Ida, a gentleman snorted. He tapped his cane on the floor impatiently.

Rose Ida, still directing traffic, said, sweetly, "Have we taken your place? Come." She escorted him to the left side of the clinic where a young black mother was juggling an infant and a two-year-old. "There you go," she said, seating the old gentleman. She turned to other patients, greeting each by name. "How are you feelin', Flora? Oh, Mr. Jones, I haven't seen you lately. The doctor will be with you shortly." She crossed the room, her voice rising in volume as she worked her way down the row of patients, closing in on Dr. Otis and his nurse.

The nurse bustled over, all starched and outdone, said, "Mrs. Tisdale, please."

Rose Ida said, misunderstanding perfectly, "Thank you for seein' Raephine so promptly."

Mozelle, still standing at the receptionist's desk, covered her mouth with her hand. Kate went over and said, "Let's wait outside."

Mozelle said, laughing behind her hand, "Do let's, before I pee in my pants."

As Mozelle and Kate descended the clinic stairs, Mr. Wallace started up. The two women did not give way. The fat man backed down.

Kate was the first to speak. "Mr. Wallace, how are you today?" she said.

Kate watched his face flicker with a kaleidoscope of pinks and reds. He reached for his shirt pocket. He let out a puff of breath. Kate could smell the nicotine and sweat.

Kate said, "Whatever is the matter?

Mr. Wallace patted his pants pocket with agitation, "I lost somethin'," he answered. "My rent book. I saw it last the day Mr. Leroy died." He touched his shirt pocket again.

Mozelle told him briskly, "Well, if you left it there, it probably burned up. You are such a good business man, I am sure you transcribed everythin' for your bookkeeper. It shouldn't be a problem replacin' the information."

"Oh," said Kate. "I know what you are looking for."

His face relaxed. "Do you have my rent book?" He took a step up toward her. "Do you have it?"

Kate reached in to her purse and drew out a red memo book.

He snatched it, eagerly flipping pages. His face fell. "What the—?"

Kate continued smoothly, "Oh, you may have it. I bought it yesterday— to write down my shopping list. It's brand new! There is something pleasing about making a fresh start, isn't there?"

Rose Ida and Raephine joined them on the steps. "Dr. Otis is such a lovely man," Rose Ida said. "Don't trouble yourself about Raephine, Mr. Wallace. Dr. Otis has fixed her up with her prescription. She has a place to live and a new job. Raephine can't wait to take Mrs. Geech's cast-iron skillet after old Mr. Trouble. What do you think Mr. Wallace, Raephine goin' have to take on anymore trouble?"

Kate finally got that sweet southern smile just right.

MOZELLE'S MARKET

Last week a man
was shot at the fruit stand.
It could have been me.
If I were to die
among the apples and the peaches
down by the watermelon
my nose in the sawdust,
bleeding like a broken jar of honey—
well, the fruit flies
would sing praises.

Photo by Howard R Harris

KATE'S PROGRESS

Floyd
1:00 PM

Oh, my sweet Ted, who art in heaven, watch over our little house. This day, I flee Hurricane Floyd with Mozelle, Rose Ida, and the standard poodle named after her late husband. We are three widows escaping the winds of the storm. If I meet you in heaven this day, I want to explain beforehand how I died in Elijah Landing's spare squad car, with the residents of three states parked along every inch of I-95 and I-26.

We are getting a late start. The *good dog* (Rose Ida calls it that, not me) decides it isn't going. Under the porch out back, it digs in where the lattice is broken. That was one of the jobs you forgot to do. I'm not blaming or nagging, Ted. The Lord called. You answered.

Rose Ida doesn't offer to kneel down to coax the dog out. Blowing smooches is the best she can do, her lipstick staining her teeth. Her perm so curly, the back of her head matches the dog's top knot, the same shade of gray. She's wearing white shorts, a man's white shirt, with a black bikini top underneath.

Ted, my dearest, I will never name an animal after you. It has her husband's eyes and a moustache. Rose Ida says it can't be Aubrey. Aubrey was a fireman. This poodle dog is a postman. It stops at every mailbox to pee. You would never consent to return to this life as a dog. But Aubrey? He loved Rose Ida so.

We escape with Mozelle driving wildly in the Crown Vic squad car. I just grab my hurricane bag as she hits the siren. Mozelle smells of persistence and passion, all shrimp and old bay. You know, she started out as a shrimper girl. Now as mayor of Elijah's Landing, she waits to make sure the shrimpers ice down yesterday's catch at the market and truck it out. She attends to all of her civic duties. How do you prepare enough for a storm as strong as Hugo or stronger? It is tracking straight for Elijah's Landing. We could lose our little house, but Mozelle could lose the whole town.

Forgive me. I left everything in the house. My purse is stuffed with tag ends, torn envelopes, peppermints, and my little red memo book. It is my burden. Oh, Ted, this is my life now. I can't seem to remember anything. Lists. I make lists. Then lose them.

I can't remember taking a journey without you except for my pilgrimage across the Pacific fifty-four years ago. I take this day those memories. Today I set out just as I did on December 18, 1945. The hospital ship *Rescue*, slid under the Golden Gate Bridge, headed for you, my love, in Hawaii. You, in your new uniform, a newly promoted warrant officer, took me to live in a bungalow on the beach. We had our heaven, blooming in the aftermath of war.

About 3:00 pm

The first thing I am putting on today's list: never ride with a dog. The poodle nudges me, looking for the peppermints. Shortly, it will want to inspect and water the tires. It has taken us three hours to drive the sixteen miles from the town line to the intersection at Gardens Corner. Mozelle says the governor ordered up a thousand National Guardsmen. There are certainly a lot of them—wilting in their uniforms. It looks like war. To save fuel, nobody is running the car air conditioners, but already we have seen cars off the road, hoods up and steaming.

We pass the *slough of despond* on the road to Yemassee. Leafless, ghostly white oaks stand in the Spartina grass. The tide is high. As we go by the ruins of the Sheldon Church, Rose Ida reminds me of Tecumseh Sherman's dark deeds. She looks back at me as if it were my fault, being of that stripe. That's me, your little woman from Boston, so forgetful in times of panic she forgets where she *pahks* her *r*'s.

Mozelle is talking on the police radio. Our brave son is acting emergency manager. He sounds a lot like you. My heart lurches to hear him speak. He says the bridges to the outlying islands will be closed at 7:00 p.m.

A National Guardsman flags us down at the Yemassee turnoff. He says the tracks ahead are blocked but to drive on the shoulder. He gets in the back, sitting next to me. I smell the starch and sweat on his uniform. A loving hand has been at work with an iron, for as he leaned forward to talk to Mozelle, there were still creases in his pants.

You never had me iron your uniforms after the first time. You were my gallant sailor, born fifty miles back of the Memphis Post Office. I was your prim New England bride who left scorch marks on the back of your white uniform. Not a word from you but kisses. After that, you sent uniforms to the laundry for heavy starch and knife creases.

Rose Ida says, "Oh Lord, keep Floyd out to sea. This here evacuation is a tri-state confabulation. Everyone just about to be scruffin', scroggin', flip-floppin' off this road. Then ker-boom. Ain't nobody goin' to get ahead of this storm. Nary one of us goin' to reach higher ground. We'll all be caught on the Interstate or in the ditches."

"Yes ma'am. It's one hot mess," the guardsman agrees.

I say, "Maybe the safest place is home."

It takes another hour to drive the five miles to the railroad crossing. We are all silent until we let the guardsman out where a car has run out of gas. He orders a few men to push the car off the tracks and into the grass on the other side.

Mozelle gets out, talking to the stranded motorists. One couple has kin up the road. Mozelle brings them back to the squad car, carrying nothing but an ice cooler. The old guy gets a look at Rose Ida. Rose Ida has her shirt unbuttoned, fanning herself with a map. She shows a good bit of leg, spider veins and all, as she scooches over the gear box.

The old lady makes sure to get in with Rose Ida. The man squeezes in with the poodle and me. The dog licks his face then backs up trying to sit in my lap. I push back. They turn out to be related to Mozelle—but everybody is related to Mozelle now.

The old man says to me, "I remember back …what was it? … the storm of 1939 or '40? Down towards Little Dog Key. Nobody evacuated. Your cousin rode that there mule of his over the island, warnin' folk. Remember, Mae Etta? It done tore the roof off the Praise House. But down at the Landings—nothing but wind and rain."

He taps his wife's shoulder, leaning forward to get a good look down Rose Ida's shirt "Remember Hurricane Gracie? We sat on our mattress in the hallway. None of this evacuation mess."

I hear Mae Etta cough, a sound deep in her chest, a soft warning. Olin sits back, reddening. "The Lord brought Gracie in at low tide."

It doesn't seem to matter to Rose Ida. She says, "Mae Etta, you're getting Oldheimer's Disease? Miss Mae Etta says she can't remember if she locked her door."

I answer, "Did I lock mine?"

Rose Ida doesn't hear me. She's off on another tangent. "Mozelle, Mozelle, call the Department of Emergency Management." She crams extra long ee's into each big word. "I feel it in my bones. That storm's taking a jog to the east. See what they think."

The poodle dog leaps to the front seat. I have some breathing room only for a minute as the old gentleman shifts his ice cooler from his lap to the space between us. He asks, "Anyone for a Co'-Cola?"

Rose Ida hollers in all three flavors of taking the good Lord's name in vain, diluted a bit by the God-Bless-You following. She grabs the drink and consumes it with such cries of rapture and wriggling of body parts that it's sinful.

I bite my lip so I don't utter something un-Christian.

Mozelle brakes involuntarily with a few words that rhyme with fire truck.

"Please, language!" I do my best. Now they are laughing at me.

Mozelle makes the radio call. "Rose Ida wants to know if the storm has turned? Ten-four?"

"We're waiting for the next advisory." It's our son, conceived in paradise, managing this hell of a ride. He says, "Tell Mrs. Tisdale she left her door wide open. I sent someone over to check for looting. Where y'all at?"

I correct him automatically. "Where are you?"

"Tell Mamma I heard that."

Mozelle says, "We are just over the tracks at Yemassee. It's a long wait at the I-95 ramp."

"Doomed," Rose Ida yells at him. "We are all doomed. Let's go back so we can die in our own beds."

Early Branch
6:00 PM

The squad car is at a standstill. The poodle whimpers and jumps back on Mr. Olin's lap. The dog hangs its head out the window, tongue lolling. Mr. Olin pours a little Coca-Cola in a paper cup. The dog laps eagerly.

I see a gas station on the left. The sign outside says "No Gas," but there are three port-a-potties over on the grass, each with its little line of evacuees. Bless *somebody*.

When I come out, I see the squad car is gone. I spot its tail end round the back. Rose Ida sneaks out of the back door of the country store. "Mae Etta remembered her cousin on her father's side runs this place," she tells me. "Nice ladies room, just for customers." She rattles a bag of corn chips and another Coke.

Mae Etta has a couple of cans of Vienna sausage and a loaf of bread. She grins. "Lucy Ann and her husband closed the front door. They ain't got much left to sell. They is stayin' put in the apartment above the store. Things get rough, they can go and get in the beer cooler. When the power goes off, the cooler won't be cold. The beer might get warm, but beer is beer. They got plenty of room if y'all want to stop. Olin and I are."

They left the ice box in the squad car for us. Rose Ida opens the lid of the can of sausage and feeds the poodle one little piggy toe at a time. "You want one?" she asks graciously.

Mozelle and I decline. The dog licks out the can, and Rose Ida wipes her hands. I hear another can pop. Ted, she's popping the top of a beer can. I pray most earnestly, watching Rose Ida drink her beer.

Rose Ida says, "Don't be such a Beulah."

Rose Ida passes the can to Mozelle who takes the final swig. Then Rose Ida pops another can.

Now the dog is a problem. Having eaten, it is ready for a walk. It winks and prods me with his nose. Whiskers quiver. It gives little enquiring yips. I say to Mozelle, "Let me take the dog for a walk. We'll walk forward. We can make better time than the car."

There is a ditch on both sides of the road, so the traffic can't use the shoulder. People in the cars wave and speak. Some of them sit on the hoods or open tailgates. We walk the midline. The dog is nervous, keeping his nose at my knee. We come to a grassy driveway, and we angle off into the field. I am wary, but the dog is pleased and does his duty with modesty. The wind has come up. The sky is uneasy, with a greenish cast.

Train tracks parallel the road. I stand between the crossties, looking in each direction. I see the signal on the line, red in one direction, green in the other. I wonder if the police car could ride the rails west and out of the path of Hurricane Floyd.

I traveled on tracks like these after the war was over. Pa sent me on my way in style: fox stole, roses, and kisses; his only daughter on her way to meet a husband so far away. How you, my sweet Ted, managed to get me aboard that hospital ship, I will never know. I never even questioned it.

Now the dog makes a large circle, its radius the length of his leash. He is well in the broom straw. He flushes out a wren huddled in the sedge and blue-eyed grass. I watch its jerky flight as the usually querulous bird wings silently. The bird takes shelter in a nearby tree. The wind changes direction, rippling through the pasture grasses; then it's still. I see a patch of blue sky. It appears and then is gone. It is very quiet. I no longer hear bird or insect sounds. Even the conversations of the stranded drivers and passengers stop. Everyone watches the southeastern horizon where the sky is now copper, as if a smokeless fire is burning just out of sight.

Suddenly I think of ticks. I call the dog. It comes eagerly. I realize I have used its name. "Aubrey, come."

There is a great crack of thunder. The dog barks, pulls on the lead. I totter along, losing my shoe. I slip at the edge of the ditch. My arms flail to keep my balance, but I have reached a terrible tipping point. Down I go, face into the ditch. In the last falling second, I turn, so now I lay with my left cheek in the goo. I take a long, shaky breath.

Ted, I call you, and you don't come.

The dog comes, a dirty poodle dog with its chin and paws dyed mahogany brown, peat-like strands of muck hanging from its flanks. Aubrey, a ding-dong, blessed poodle dog, gives me a kiss on the nose. I sit up and realize my chin and my hands are identically stained. My pants soak up scummy water. Mosquitoes rise and attack. As I sit, I hear cars starting up and pulling away.

"Wait," I call. Abandoned in a ditch, I will die here as Rose Ida predicted. I try to stand, but pain shoots through my ankle. The storm is in my head and in my heart. The lightning flashes through my soul. Then the thunder comes. It rains. It rains. It rains.

Who will suffer my foot to be moved, Ted?

I will. I will. I will rise.

I grab for the leash. "Come," I call to the dog. The dog thinks I am just playing a game. It barks. Ted, when I fall in a ditch, why can't my companion be Lassie?

Digging in with my bare toes, I lean on the dog and get to my knees. I rise, one leg crooked like the great blue heron.

"Mozelle," I shout. "Rose Ida. Come and get this dog." It barks cheerfully. If that poodle dog were mine, I would call it "O Be Joyful."

My friends comfort and keep me. They tend to my ankle and swaddle me in a sheet. The dog circles me, touching my knee with its nose, and whimpers as I hop back to the squad car. Mozelle stows me in the backseat. Rose Ida clucks sweet platitudes and tells me not to cry.

Oh, I cry. I cry for you. You are gone. You cannot answer. I must go through the wicket gate. I must walk the straight and narrow without a companion. I must and I will.

The dog attends me, its face close to mine. I turn my face to the seat back. I feel the dog touch me with its paw.

We are going home. The squad car rocks as Mozelle turns the car around, weaving around the out-bound cars. It is raining heavily, the wipers thump as they clear the windshield. I see the oncoming lights. After awhile, traffic thins. Instead, I see the silent lightning. I hear the sound of the railroad tracks as we rumble across them.

All at once, I smell the *pluff* mud. We must be near the Whale Branch. So near home and the little house we shared. How could I have left it so carelessly?

"O Be Joyful," I tell the dog. He smells boggy and wet, but I do not care. I see our home, a beacon in the rainy, windy night. All else is dark in Elijah's Landing. All else is dark except our dear little house, Ted.

Our son has an emergency generator going. Coffee is up. The house is full of young men in turn-out gear and T-shirts. I am so proud our son has taken charge. In the morning, I will make breakfast as best I can. I will tie on my apron and look to see what is in my pantry and in my deep-dive freezer.

Rose Ida steers me to the bathroom to wash, handing me a water jug and a candle. She calls directions through the bathroom door. When I fall into our own bed, I say one last prayer of acceptance. For a moment, I think I hear you, Ted.

Hurricane Floyd passes away east and north. Our little house on Catbrier Lane is in the center of the universe. I hear the rain. For a moment, it feels as if you are sleeping beside me, a warm but comforting presence. As I roll over I realize it is the poodle dog, O Be Joyful.

Photo by Marge Boyle

HURRICANE SEASON

June, too soon.
July, stand by.
August, look out you must.
September, remember.
October, all over.
November, except Ida.

      —Old Saying

Photo by Marge Boyle

THE MARINE CORPS BIRTHDAY STORM

NOVEMBER 10, 2009
IDA

Rose Ida Tisdale, at ninety-six, was as happy as a chicken leg on a fire ant mound. She had run all the doctors into the ground, and the nurses were ready to up her morphine so they could take vitals without Rose Ida hoo-hallowing questions about her release. Keeping her in the bed was why Camille McReady pulled the night watch, or hurricane watch. She knew Rose Ida wasn't going to die in the night. Rose Ida was not one to miss a hurricane moon when the clouds lifted.

"The General," said Rose Ida, "would never approve of a hurricane on November the tenth. What do you wear to the Marine Corps Birthday Ball? A slicker and—what's that called? A hoodie?"

Laughing, Camille paid homage to her grandmother, with a nod. "A hospital gown, Grandma. I have a pair of panties in my purse."

Rose Ida huffed, picking at the neckline of her hospital outfit. She hated it when Camille called her that. There was a time she insisted on being addressed as "Auntie" in the good old Southern way.

Her friends called the old lady Hurricane Sister. She knew all the hurricane stats and the proper responses to tales of disaster. She loved a good fire. Total destruction kept her going for weeks. She was also the source of the South's best gossip and set the highest standards of behavior.

She preached long and loud about Camille's choice of husband. "It's not done. People will talk."

Rose Ida's dominion that November evening consisted of her hospital room. Her life was bounded by windows where she had a good view of the parking lot. The nurses' station formed the other boundary; beyond that were the often unguarded elevators. Most everyone assumed she couldn't get very far with an oxygen line, an IV drip, a walker, and a nearly naked behind.

"Now, Grandma," Camille said to get her back up. "Don't trouble yourself. It's just a tropical storm, just a little wind and rain. Besides, it's still in the gulf." She smoothed the sheet on the hospital bed.

Rose Ida pointed an accusatory finger at the rain-spattered window. "Hurricane Ida, what kind of name is that?"

"About as good a name as Hurricane Camille," she grinned, forcing the dimples and batting her blue eyes. She had been named for the big storm in 1969. As a toddler, Camille told strangers her name was "Don't Touch That." Now that she was forty, she ought to say Rose Ida, and answered to Camille McReady. But she didn't.

"And why are you bringing up the General at this late date? I thought he was just a lieutenant colonel."

"Fool girl," Rose Ida said.

Fool girl was what she answered to. In those two words, Rose Ida told her Camille had grown plump and self-satisfied with her husband and all his cars in the yard.

"Major, I hear," Raephine Blue said, bringing in the dinner tray. Raephine was Rose Ida's longtime companion and caregiver. She was a brown wren of a woman. She tilted her chin up to look taller, prouder, a war woman, an African queen. They were both here for the duration.

"Major Pain-in-the-Ass," Rose Ida mumbled. She plucked at the sheet and then reached for her makeup kit on the bedside table.

What Rose Ida wanted to do was flounce off to the ball instead of languishing in the stormy night. Southern girls should dance with boys in lovely uniforms, courtly and so fine.

"Get me out of here. Where is that man?" She called for her second husband as often as for the General, her first love. One of them was supposed to rescue her.

"Grandma," Camille said. "Grandpa died in 1996."

"She knows that," Raephine said. "Somewhere in her memory, she knows. Don't trouble her with the details. She knows, just not right this minute. But she remembers the General."

Camille hated it when Raephine went into her subservient maid routine. She needed to mouth that old lady and roll those eyes. She needed to say, "About that ole general, get down to it. We's waitin' for the juicy bits."

Raephine tried to place the tray in front of Rose Ida, but she pushed her away. With a sigh, Raephine placed it on the bedside table. She pulled out a bleach-filled wipe and cleaned the hospital table.

"Get the edges," Rose Ida said. She pointed out missed spots. "Hand me my sanitizer."

"What else can I get you?" Camille honeyed up her accent and lifted the lid over the dish. Steam brought the smell of the food. "You have minced chicken, mashed potatoes, and lime Jell-O."

As she cleaned her hands with gelled alcohol, Rose Ida said, "Just bring my cedar box." Her nails, painted a girlish pink with French tips, contrasted with the knuckles, swollen and freckled with age. She inspected her hands and blew out a breath. "Or get me out of here."

"I'll get it. Just tell me where it is," Camille said. "You eat now. When I get back I want to see a clean plate and a good report."

"Fool girl, look under the bed," Rose Ida said. She raised her voice. "And I hate lime Jell-O!"

"She wants the *hurricane box*," Raephine said, "You know. What you take come *h-e-double-hockey sticks* or high water."

Camille knew good and well what she wanted. "I think Husband got another car. He said it would be a surprise." The two words in the sentence were sure to annoy her—*husband* and *car*.

"My hell-or-high-water cedar box," Rose Ida repeated in a scornful falsetto. "All I want to do is say bad words and dance. Remember *my* car." She heaved the dessert into a trash can at her bedside.

Camille knew that car.

"Hush, now," said Raephine. "Y'all just stay here with me. I'll be right here, quiet. I won't bother you none. You don't have to eat neither."

As Rose Ida scooped the mashed potato into a mountain, she said, "Sit down, Raephine. I want to tell you a story." She aimed a spoonful of potato at the trash can. When the potato hit the plastic liner and slid down on the gelatin, she raised her fingers. "Two points."

Camille left the room but leaned against the wall outside to listen. Her husband could get the damned cedar box. She was tired. Their roles were reversed. Rose Ida was the one who used to set the limit. *No. Don't touch that. You can't. The General this. The General, oh law.*

"I would like to hear your story," Raephine said. She took a tattered sachet bag out of her pocket and held it to her nose. The scent of rosemary wafted around the room, as she motioned for Camille to return. Camille shook her head and ducked out of Rose Ida's line of sight. Raephine sat down.

All her life she had listened to the stories. The General was rich and the divorce bitter. The child of the divorce, Camille's mother, would lose her inheritance if she sought out her birthmother. And yet the unwed daughter returned to Rose Ida. Everything about Camille was hush, hush. Now she was the one saying no. *What am I going to do? Let her live out her time here under protest or take her home. Where does that leave me in the world?* She wanted to scream. *What about Camille?*

"My mamma said I was a floozy and would come to no good. I bobbed my hair and ran around," Rose Ida said.

Folding her hands into her lap, Raephine said, "Did some of that myself."

"It wasn't done. People talked. I ran off. Then the war started." Rose Ida frowned and narrowed her eyes. "Raephine, how long you been taking care of me? Since my husband died. Oh law, and that."

"Not me," Raephine said. "You be the boss of yourself. Never mind poor Raephine."

Rose Ida asked, "Where did Camille go?" Pointing to the froth of pink and purple on her walker, she said, "Give me my bed jacket." Her finger trembled as she gestured.

Raephine gave Camille a long, hard look, and then she helped Rose Ida tame the silky material and threaded her bony arms into the sleeves. The IV monitor started to ping.

"Hurry up," Rose Ida said, "Let me see. Let me see her go." Rose Ida struggled, swinging her legs over the side of the bed, legs of straw, wobbly and striated with purple veins so that she looked like she wore gypsy-crazy stockings to match the frou-frou bed jacket. By the time she got to the window, she was panting and puffing. When Raephine offered the plastic tubing, the hiss of oxygen, Rose Ida pushed it away. "What color car did she get? Can you see?"

Camille gave up. "I'm right here, Grandma."

A nurse bustled in, alarmed at the chirping and buzzing coming from the medical instruments at her station. She helped Rose Ida. "There now, Mrs. Tisdale. Hop back into bed."

"If I could hop, I'd be hopping out of here," Rose Ida said, and when she caught her breath, "I had a job in the laundry and lived in a boarding house."

The nurse tucked the hospital corners. She was a new one who didn't know that she was on soft *pluff* mud as far as Rose Ida was concerned. The nurse asked, "When was that, sweetie?"

"It was 1943. We leaned out of the boardin' house window watchin' the cars. Girls stayed, bunked up three to four in a room, nightshift, swing shift, day shift sharin' the rooms. We picked a car and wished. An official US Navy car turned into the street. It could be bad news. An officer and a chaplain meant a boy missin'—or worse. The married girls started to cry. Two sailors got out and waved. Good news! Someone on leave. We waved back. Not our sailor, not our jarhead."

"Roll over a bit, honey," said the nurse. She and Raephine adjusted the bed pad and then, in a tandem motion, pulled up the covers before the nurse tucked her side in. "There you go. Get some rest, you hear."

"Oh law," Rose Ida said and made a face. She threw off the blanket and sheet. "He was a handsome boy. I brought him his shirts, starched heavy enough to stand up and salute. I said, 'Here you go, General.' He blushed. He was only a second lieutenant, a flier, but he liked that. He remembered me." She rolled her eyes; her cheeks colored.

"Every week, while his ship was in port he came. I said, 'Here, you go, General. I sure could use a Coke. Go down the corner and get me one.' Good looking enough to be a general. Walked like a general and talked sweet, sweet talk."

Later, Camille's husband brought the hurricane box. It was one of those souvenir chests. This one was from Florida, painted on top with aging flamingos. All Hurricane Sisters have a box or a suitcase ready from June first to the end of November. Like Girl Scouts, hurricane sisters were ready for any hurricane evacuation.

Rose Ida pulled up her knees so they formed two sheet mountains around the box. She held up a photograph. "That was your mother, and that was you," she said. "Your grandpa took the picture the day daughter showed up. She had no use for you. But remember, your grandpa and I painted the stars on your ceiling—and the moon. You were our hurricane child, into everything." Rose Ida tucked the photograph into her gown.

Frowning at the dust on the lid, she wiped the rounded top with the edge of the sheet. "He said *she* was his sister," Rose Ida said.

A soft sound, a nickering sigh, came from Raephine. She slid into a kneeling position next to Rose Ida, who stroked the younger woman's head. In the dim light, her hand was pale in Raephine's dark hair. Their voices were soft and confessional.

Camille tried to keep quiet, but kept punctuating Rose Ida's story with questions. "The General's sister?"

"Hush now, Miss Rose Ida," Raephine said.

She drew a breath. Her voice strengthened. "He borrowed a car to drive out to Elkton, but we had a fight. I was sure he was seeing another girl, that he'd lied. I threw the ring at him. He said *she* was his sister. Then he shipped out."

Camille was shocked. "You didn't marry him?"

"I bought a gold band when I realized I was pregnant. I was alone. Still there were lots of girls like me workin', alone. She *was* his sister...."

"What about the baby?"

Tears filled her eyes. She raked her hands through her hair. "The baby.

I couldn't deal with a baby. Oh law, his sister came for her. I gave her away! She grew up cold, Camille. She grew up hard."

"But she grew up and became my mother."

"Little hurricane child," Rose Ida said, "when you asked, 'Who is my mamma? Tell me about my real mamma,' I threw stones on the beach and told stories as hard as baking powder biscuits."

"You said my mamma flew away over the moon. I knew you were foolin' me. But none of those things matters now."

"Did I ever tell you I loved you?"

"You said, 'Fool, girl. Don't touch that'," Camille laughed. "But we had fun. You always said 'give life a pat and a promise. The ironing can wait.' All of this is long past, forty years gone. I'm near as old as you then. Did you think I never looked in that box?"

"Conjure for me, Raephine," Rose Ida said and grabbed Raephine's hand. "Take the spell off. Camille can't go along like me. She needs to be free."

"I don't mess with root, Miss Rose Ida. You know that," Raephine said.

"You do." Rose Ida was adamant. "You got *goofer* dust in that little rag bag. I know you do. Take hex off before I die. I don't want anything taintin' Camille. It was *my* sin. Make it go away!"

After a long moment, Raephine drew out her sachet and passed it over the top of the cedar chest. The scent filled the room, rosemary for remembrance.

"Here are his letters," Rose Ida said.

Taking out a small wooden pin case from her pocket, Raephine counted out nine straight pins. She pierced all four corners, using a different pin for each envelope. Then she carefully counted the pins again and put them away. She dusted the inside of the box. Once more, the smell intensified. Raephine closed the lid. "Give Miss Rose Ida a bleach wipe," she told Camille.

Rose Ida wiped the outside and the inside of the box. Then she cleaned her hands.

"*Wash away,*" Raephine began a hymn, low and husky. "*Wash away sin and sorrow weeping,*" she sang. "*We ain't got long to stay here....*"

"All the storm warnings have been canceled. The moon is out,

Grandma." Camille decided what to do—She unplugged the IV monitor and gently removed the needle from Rose Ida's arm. Then she pulled a pair of silk panties out of her purse. "Get dressed Grandma. We are gettin' out of here."

Her husband had parked a white, 1968 Olds Toronado convertible with red interior at the back exit of the hospital, near the Dumpsters. Rose Ida was amazed as Camille *wanged* the wheelchair around the corner. Settled into the backseat of the big white car, she cooed. "It's just like the one I had back in the day."

"Husband bought it for you, Grandma," Camille said. She persuaded Raephine to sit up front. "Like white folks."

"Look at the moon. Look at the moon," Rose Ida cried. The moon was *demilune*, half a bright white cheese or a goddess's lantern. When Camille got to the Marine Corps Crossing Bridge, Rose Ida cajoled her to stop and watch the moon's face dabble in the water.

Camille parked the big car on the bridge and turned off the headlights.

"I can't lie before the moon," Rose Ida said. She had one last story to tell. "There wasn't a baby."

"What do you mean, 'no baby'?"

Her voice was low. "I got rid of it."

Camille let her head crash forward onto the steering wheel and took a deep angry breath before turning around to face her. Determined not to cry, she asked, "Then Grandma, who is my mother?"

"I met a hippie girl crying in the Piggly Wiggly. Some damned Marine got himself killed in Vietnam. There was a war on, you know. I told her not to do what I did and to give you to me."

"You got me at the Piggly Wiggly store?"

"Sixty-nine cents a pound."

"Grandma," Camille screamed, her voice rising to a hog-calling pitch. As the echo died away, she gave a snot-filled snort ... and then began to laugh. "For sixty-nine cents, want to bet I get booked for old lady–napping?" she said.

Raephine and Camille exchanged glances. Then with two minds in one accord and with that old lady hoo-hallowing in the backseat, they heaved the hell-or-high-water box over the side of the bridge.

Well, everything was as plain as the last sliced tomato on a plate. Camille knew who she was—nobody's child. She was nobody's storm and nobody's trouble. She owed nothing to the old lady who had picked her up like produce. She was Camille McReady, a real bargain. It was deliciously juicy.

They parked there more than a minute with the moon, maybe more than two, maybe a lifetime. Rose Ida struggled up to sit on the back of the seat like the beauty queen she claimed she was. She waved, the waning moon shining on her face and her breasts.

A cop pulled up, the blue lights of his patrol car washing over them. They stifled laughter. Rose Ida slid onto the seat, a proper lady, but hiccupping. The deputy was a young one, the size a fisherman would throw back. He knew them, toting them up by name. "Mrs. Tisdale, Mrs. McReady." He left out Raephine. "Are you ladies all right?"

Raephine spoke up, "We are watching the moon."

"Right," Camille told the deputy, "We just tossed a case of moonshine."

Knowing all their histories, he laughed. Then he leaned against the broad expanse of the car's hood and looked at the moon. Finally, he pointed the way to the other side of the bridge. "Get on up the road, now, you hear?" he said.

As the cop pulled away, Rose Ida said, "Oh law, now that's a handsome boy."

Camille took Rose Ida home in her convertible.

Now Rose Ida never saw the moon again in this life. Rose Ida died two days later in Camille's old room, where she had painted the night sky on the ceiling forty years before. Camille tended her not from obligation or by her command, but with a quick and open heart. Around her Camille's kids ran riot and husband tinkered with cars without reprimand. Her last breath came easy and with a grin.

Six long months, Camille watched the moon wax and wane, praying Rose Ida had charmed her way into heaven. The hurricane season came once more. It didn't seem the same without her directing predictions and preparations. She probably ordered the lesser angels around some, cataloging storm and cloud. Perhaps she looked the Lord in the eye and said, "Oh law, you see that there house with all them cars in the yard? The one in the beautiful town by the sea? Don't touch that."

Photo by Marge Boyle

BACKGROUND

THE HURRICANES

    1959—Gracie

    1969—Camille

    1979—David

    1989—Hugo

    1999—Floyd

    2009—Ida

THE COME-HERES

    Kate and Ted Forester

        Sissy Forester Merrill, Kate and Ted's daughter

        J. T., John Thomas or Little Man—their son

    Rose Ida and Aubrey Tisdale

        Rose Ida's granddaughter, Camille Tisdale McReady

        The General, Rose Ida's first husband whose rank rises with the passing of time. (Nobody's supposed to talk about him.)

        Rose Ida's Lost daughter, unnamed and disgraced. (Nobody's supposed to talk about her either. They do.)

THE BEEN-HERES

Clara Blue, the maid

Leroy Blue, the vegetable man (Nobody's supposed to talk about his other job.)

Leroy Blue Jr.—Mr. Leroy's son, killed in Vietnam

Raephine Blue—Mr. Leroy's daughter-in-law and a real good cook (Nobody's supposed to talk about her other skills.)

The Possum Child, Janey—Raephine's daughter

Grady and Tillis Geech, the shrimpers (Nobody is supposed to talk about where Tillis went.)

Mozelle Geech Seabrook—Tillis Geech's daughter—married to Gunny Seabrook (killed in Vietnam)

Prudence, Patience, and Petula Seabrook—Mozelle's daughters

Conway ("Connie boy") Eustis—cousin to the Seabrooks and the Geeches, a writer from somewhere else (Nobody talks about his books … yet.)

J. C. Fewell returned to the Low Country in 2001 after spending many years as a special education teacher in Prince George's County, Maryland, as well as a fictional writing teacher at Prince George's County Community College in Largo, Maryland. She published her first story, "Uncle Sugar's Finest," in 1990 and is a proud survivor of Hurricane Gracie.